LITTLE MEXICO

LITTLE MEXICO

CATHIE JOHN

JOURNEYBOOK PRESS

LITTLE MEXICO

JOURNEYBOOK PRESS
is an imprint of
CC Comics / CC Publishing
P.O. Box 542, Loveland, OH 45140-0542
ccpub@worldnet.att.net

Logo designed by Steve Del Gardo

ISBN 0-9634183-7-8

First Edition: 2000

10 9 8 7 6 5 4 3 2 1

Printed in the United States by:
Morris Publishing
3212 East Highway 30
Kearney, NE 68847
1-800-650-7888

THIS IS A WORK OF FICTION BASED ON ACTUAL CONDITIONS AND EVENTS THAT EXISTED AND OCCURRED IN NEWPORT, KENTUCKY (AKA LITTLE MEXICO) IN 1943.

LITTLE MEXICO HAS BEEN POPULATED WITH A COMBINATION OF REAL AND IMAGINED PEOPLE, ALL OF WHOM INTERACT AND SPEAK AT THE AUTHORS' WHIM. THOUGH WORDS HAVE BEEN PUT IN THE MOUTHS OF HISTORICAL FIGURES, THE AUTHORS HAVE NOT ALTERED WHAT THE RESEARCH REVEALED ABOUT THEIR INDIVIDUAL CHARACTERS AND ACTIONS.

LITTLE MEXICO

1

"THE DAYS OF THE MOM 'N POP operations are over, Jimmy. They're sitting on a prime spot down there in Newport, so move 'em out. *Capeesh?*"

"Yeah, I capeesh. I'll get Lester on it right away." Jimmy "the Shiv" Turelli left the back room at Meyer's Delicatessen with his marching orders from Moe Dalitz. Not exactly the ritziest of joints, but that's where the Big Four of the Cleveland Syndicate—Moe, Sam Tucker, Louis Rothkopf, and Morris Kleinman—held some of their business meetings. And this had been an important one. Sam even came all the

11

way up from Kentucky to attend it.

Jimmy picked up his usual order of pastrami, sliced thin and packed in butcher's paper, from Arnie who lived behind the counter.

"See ya, Jimmy."

"Ciao, Arnie."

Jimmy would rather be working for Italians, but Elliot Ness had busted up the Mayfield Road Mob, leaving the Jew boys to run this part of the country. So that's the way it goes in Cleveland. He grabbed a dill pickle out of the barrel on his way out.

Sam was going back to Newport in a day or two—he'd moved there a couple of years ago in order to supervise day-to-day operations of the Beverly Hills Country Club, their biggest casino. Jimmy would like to drive down with him and personally bust Carl Jules' ass, but the boys in the back room were going for more sophisticated methods and wanted everything handled business-like.

Okay, so letters go out to Buck Brady at the Primrose Club and Carl Jules at The Oasis with nice offers—carrots to make those two mule-headed SOBs fall into line like the others. Yeah, he'll contact Charles Lester down in Newport. Have him write it all out nice and proper. Didn't want anything in black and white looking like they were being told "Pay or Die!" He'd also contact Red Masterson, their enforcer down there in Little Mexico, with orders to nudge Buck and Carl towards those carrots.

Jimmy chomped into his pickle. Those little mom 'n pop casinos weren't so small. They were swanky places raking in lots of cash, and the Syndicate didn't like competition. Didn't matter that Carl and those others had set up shop years ago. When Moe Dalitz went down, saw how much dough flowed into places like the Beverly Hills and The Oasis, he came back to Cleveland with a mind to take it all over. Shit, the boys sure did that. Except for a handful of holdouts like Carl.

This was real sweet, Jimmy thought, as he checked his reflection in the store window. He adjusted the tilt of his new twenty-five dollar fedora, and ran his fingers along its crisp brim. Jimmy had been looking forward to going after Carl Jules for a long time. He had a personal score to settle. Yeah, send the carrot by way of a letter. But if the carrot don't work, use a stick. A big pointy stick.

And Jimmy the Shiv knew just where to shove it.

——

NEWPORT, KENTUCKY

CLAUDETTE CRINGED INWARDLY AT the feel of Bruno's damp paw on her neck. She knew what he was thinking. She could feel it coming right through his claw-like fingers as they pressed in on her throat—the barely-contained desire to squeeze her windpipe until her eyes popped and her lungs gasped for air. One little squeeze. That's all it would take.

Bruno always got like this on the nights he was about to go on one of his jobs—caught up in some private world, a brutal fantasy that put him in the mood for the work ahead. Claudette never wanted to know what grizzly plans were forming in his brain.

Not that any of her other customers were all there. Most of them seemed to have their minds on something else as they banged away at her body until they were satisfied and went on their way.

She couldn't wait until he was finished. His ugly face bobbed up and down a half inch from hers. It looked like years ago someone had tried to gouge out Bruno's left cheek with a can opener. She turned away from the sight of his crooked yellow teeth and the smell of his sour breath. A moment later, Claudette heard his little grunt. *Good, he's finished.* She got up, wrapped a silk kimono around her body, and lit a cigarette.

Bruno grunted again as he put on his pants. "That was great, doll."

Yeah, sure. How the hell would you know? In and out, in and out. Stupid ugly jerk.

He finished putting on his rumpled suit and tossed a bill on the bed. "Here's something extra for you."

Claudette scooped it up. A crisp twenty. She smiled at him as he lumbered out her bedroom door. He may be an ugly jerk of a killer, but he was a generous one and a buck is a buck, and she didn't have to split this with Sophie. It would all go into her escape fund.

The gifts she got from soldiers and sailors on leave were nice, but silk robes and stockings weren't going to get her out of Newport, Kentucky.

"God, he stinks." Claudette grabbed her atomizer and spritzed the air with *Evening in Paris*—one of those gifts.

She stepped across her tiny room and threw open the window. The acrid stench pumped out by the steel mills greeted her. She wrinkled her nose in disgust. Wasn't much better out there.

A woman's laugh echoed in the street below. Claudette looked down from her second floor window and saw two women in the glow of the streetlight making their way to the corner—a couple of Rosie Riveters dressed in overalls on their way to the midnight shift. Claudette gave them a little salute. Well, every gal's gotta do her bit for God and Country. But *she* sure wasn't going to sweat on the factory line like them. She was doing her sweating for her country in between the sheets. Entertaining the troops. Claudette laughed at her own thought. She was pumping up more than a soldier's morale and making a helluva lot more money at it too, that was for damn sure.

She flicked her cigarette butt out the window and, folding one leg underneath her, sat down on the cracked leather hassock and propped her elbows on the windowsill. Directly across the street from her were the neon lights of the Glenn Rendezvous. It was almost midnight and the gambling club was doing its usual business. Even though a smaller sign said HOTEL, and there were rooms available on the third floor, no guests stayed overnight. Most of them only made it up to the second floor, riding up the secret elevator hidden behind the paneled wall in the lobby.

Claudette watched a couple of men in business suits shuffle out of the club with the usual stooped posture that marked them.

"Losers." She snorted in disgust. That's almost all she ever saw coming out of Pete Schmidt's bustout joint.

The lobby doors of the Glenn Rendezvous opened and a blast of dance music escaped. On the street level, customers were having a good time eating and drinking in the supper club. It was a different story up on the second floor. Claudette could imagine the grim faces of the players huddled around the tables. The room would be silent except for the muffled music from below and the clicks of loaded dice. No way anybody beat.the odds playing Razzle Dazzle.

She shook another cigarette out of its pack, lit it, and blew a smoke ring out the window into the sooty air. A view of the river and the bridges would be a helluva lot better than staring at the Glenn Rendezvous night after night. Someday, she'd take one of those bridges into Cincinnati, hop a train at Union Terminal, and not get off until it chugged into Hollywood.

Didn't seem like such a long shot, her getting into pictures. All she needed was the money to get there, and once they saw her big green eyes and pale, perfect complexion...

Claudette picked up a dog-eared copy of *Photoplay* off the floor and stared at the image of Katharine Hepburn on the cover. "If that scrawny, flat-chested broad could make it, no reason *I* can't." She threw the magazine across the room and slinked towards her own image in the mirror over her dressing table. Claudette dabbed on a fresh coat of lipstick, leaned over the dressing table showing off her deep cleavage, and pouted into the imaginary camera lens.

"Claudette?" Sophie's voice came from the hallway outside her door. "We got gentlemen guests in the parlor." The wooden floors creaked under the madam's weight as she waddled back downstairs.

Claudette pulled her silk robe across her breasts, and hugged herself. It wasn't that the night air was cold—it was remembering the feel of Bruno's fingers gliding across her throat again that made her shiver. The man had a mind to hurt people. Liked it. Liked it too much. She looked out the window one more time. Who was Bruno going to hit tonight?

Claudette squared her shoulders, shook a mass of dark curly hair off her face with a toss of her head, and strode downstairs to meet the gentlemen guests. *The losers.*

——————

"*G*ODDAMMIT, BRUNO. Stop clowning around. Let me go."

Bruno Carpella responded with a laugh as Charlie DePalma struggled with the rope binding his hands together behind his back.

Charlie kept talking. "Why you doing this to me?" Charlie had already soiled the crisply pressed trousers of his two hundred dollar suit because he knew the answer, but he couldn't believe it was happening. Not to him. Not to "Dandy" Charlie. He watched Manny dump another bag of cement into the wheelbarrow.

The dust billowed up in front of Bruno's face. He sneezed out his mouth.

Charlie felt gobs of slime hit his face.

"Sorry," Bruno said, reaching for the dress handkerchief in the breast pocket of Charlie's suit jacket. He brought it up to his nose, honked loudly into it a couple of times, then shoved the soggy linen back into place and patted the resulting bulge. "Thanks."

Charlie bit at the little fringe of a moustache adorning his upper lip. *Think fast.* "I can pay it all back, Bruno. Here. In my pocket." He indicated which side of his jacket with a shrug of his right shoulder.

Cocking an eyebrow, Bruno turned to the fourth thug

in the basement of Cooky's disorderly house. "Check him, Al."

Al leaned the shovel he was using to mix cement against the wall and quickly relieved Charlie of a thick leather wallet. "Lots of C notes in here."

Bruno sniffed. All this dust floating around made him grouchy. Now he'd been insulted with this penny ante offer. Bruno walked across the dimly lit cellar to Al's shovel, grabbed it, and spiked it into the dirt floor. He thumbed the snap brim of his hat, pushing it to the back of his head. "Charlie? What d'ya think? I'm as fucking stupid as *you* are? Put yourself in my shoes. Red Masterson gives an order—I follow through."

Charlie started trembling. Bruno smiled. *This is fun.*

Bruno walked towards him, dragging the shovel behind, and shaking his head from side to side. "Charlie, Charlie, why'd ya do it? You were supposed to be collecting for him, he trusted you. But how do you repay his trust? Skimming off the top ain't the way to do it."

Bruno walked right past him and pushed his shovel into the wheelbarrow full of wet cement. "What's the matter? You look a little cold, Charlie. Manny, roll that over a little closer."

Silently, Manny obeyed and rolled an empty oil drum on its rim over to where Charlie stood quaking in his boots.

Bruno tapped out a snappy *rat-a-tat-tat* on the metal top with his thick, yellow fingernails. "Why don't you sit in here. We'll pack you in nice and tight. Warm you up a bit."

Bruno saw a wet stain form on the front of Charlie's right pant leg, and smirked. He could see desperation in Charlie's eyes a split second before Charlie bolted for the cellar door. He didn't get more than three steps before Bruno slugged him with the shovel on the back of his head. The clang of steel against bone reverberated around the basement. Charlie was out cold.

Manny and Al caught Charlie before he hit the ground, dragged him back to the barrel, and stuffed him in, feet first. Charlie's head hung back over the rim, mouth gaping.

Bruno said, "Looks like he's waiting to have his tooth yanked."

Manny and Al snorted.

Bruno started shoveling cement into the barrel, filling it up to Charlie's chest.

Charlie groaned.

"He's coming to," Al said.

"No shit," replied Bruno. "Think I'm deaf?" He turned to his patient. "Hey, Charlie Boy, we know how you like your clothes to fit just right, so before we put you to bed, I'm making sure your nightgown is good and snug."

Bruno was getting more aroused with each shovelful he piled onto Charlie's upper torso. *What a great night.* Charlie started moving around, trying to get out of the barrel. Bruno swung his shovel and smashed Charlie upside the head. Charlie stopped squirming.

After packing the rest of the cement around Charlie's torso, until he was totally encased, Bruno announced, "Okay, let's just wait a while 'til things get quieter on the street."

Manny and Al pushed a few wooden crates together under the bare light bulb. Al pulled out a deck of cards and started dealing. "You playin', Bruno?"

"Nah." Bruno shoved his hands into his pockets, jingled some coins, and pulled out a pack of Lucky Strikes. He lit one, inhaled deeply, and blew a long stream of smoke out his nose. Bruno looked at Charlie, studying his handiwork with a feeling of deep satisfaction. As a reward for tonight's job, Red Masterson promised to give Bruno the collection duties. Thanks to the dandy in the barrel, he'd just taken his first step up the ladder in the Cleveland Syndicate's organization.

Bruno saw that the collar of Charlie's white silk shirt had soaked up the blood that trickled down his cheek from the gash on the side of his head. Bruno placed two fingers on the vein in Charlie's neck. It was still pumping.

"Can't count on this sonofabitch to stay quiet." Bruno picked up one of the paper cement mix bags and tore off a piece. He used it to scoop up a blob of partially-hardened cement that had fallen onto the floor. He opened Charlie's mouth and packed it in.

"That should do it."

AROUND 3:00 A.M., Bruno shoved Charlie's head down into the barrel and hammered the lid in place. Manny and Al laid a couple of wooden planks over the concrete cellar steps. They put the oil drum into the wheelbarrow, and pulled Charlie up the makeshift ramp and out to their truck.

They drove down Second Street, Manny in the back with their cargo, Bruno hunched over the wheel. Al, riding shotgun, peered nervously through the windshield. "Hey, Bruno," he said, "the cops still patrolling the bridge?"

"Nah. They stopped doing that. Nazis and Japs ain't gonna bomb Newport, Kentucky."

"What about the guards over on the Cincinnati side?"

Bruno glanced sideways at Al. "It's gotta be close to half a mile across that river. They ain't gonna see shit in the dark. Besides, we're only going a couple of hundred feet to the first piling." But he clicked off the truck's headlights just in case. No sense in attracting attention.

In contrast to Second Street, still active at this time of night with customers going in and out of its brothels, a block away the riverfront was dark and deserted. Bruno brought the truck to a halt at the ramshackle dock on the banks of the Ohio River. They waited, listening to the silence broken only by the sound of three wooden rowboats, tied to the dock, making soft thuds as they banged into each other.

Bruno finally said, "Okay, let's go."

Wooden planks in place, Manny maneuvered the wheelbarrow off the back of the truck and onto the dock. It took all three of them to lift Charlie into a rowboat.

Al whispered, "It's so fucking dark I can barely see what I'm doing."

"Shut your mouth," Bruno whispered back. "What d'ya want? Fucking floodlights?"

Once they were seated in the boat, Al pushed off from the dock. As Manny picked up the oars and began rowing, Bruno said, "Stay under the bridge. Just get us to that first piling."

A series of *thumps* sounded from inside the oil drum. Bruno looked at the hammered-down lid and imagined Charlie's head thrashing from side to side, his eyes wide open, eyeballs rolling frantically in their sockets.

It took only a few minutes to get to their destination. Al dropped anchor. A good fifty feet over their heads, two cars were crossing the bridge.

Guttural noises echoed inside the metal drum.

Bruno smiled and shook his head. "No use. Nobody's gonna hear you."

Al said, "C'mon. Let's get this over with."

"What's the matter? Not having fun?" Bruno turned to Charlie and tapped him on the lid. "Nighty night."

They tucked Charlie DePalma into the muddy waters of the O—Hi—O.

2

SEPTEMBER 15

SAN DIEGO

LOGBOOK ENTRY:

A S SHORE PATROLMEN on the San Diego Naval Base, Joey Jules and I were officially responsible for guarding entrances, breaking up fights, and going into town to relieve the local police department of drunken sailors and bringing them back to base. We were good at it. In fact, we were so good, the Captain rewarded us with ten days furlough. Well, maybe we weren't that special. Maybe he gave it to us because we hadn't had any leave for the past twelve months and it was due us.

Anyway, it created a big problem for me, and I was still chewing it over when Joey and I went out on the town to hit the bars.

We pushed through the doors of one of our usual haunts. It was a smoke-filled joint. Cab Calloway was singing out of the jukebox, but I could barely hear him over the shouting and laughter.

The male clientele wasn't exactly officer material—more like swabs who'd shanghai their own brothers for a couple of bucks. The women looked a little used around the edges, too. The jukebox switched to a slow *"I'll never smile again,"* and a couple started to dance—well, it was more like a slow fondle. A game of pool was going on in the back corner.

At the bar, Joey ordered us a couple of beers and started right in getting chummy with a woman drinking one of those pink, frothy concoctions. As usual, heads swiveled and I felt eyes looking up at me.

A crusty old seadog pointed his chin at me and said, "How tall are you?"

I answered, "Six-four."

"Kinda big for a sailor. How do they fit you on board?" He scanned my white uniformed chest, looking for campaign ribbons. I don't have any.

"I'm on permanent Shore Patrol duty," I said.

"Oh. Guess you don't see any action." He lost interest and turned back to his drink.

Damn, there's times I wish I could chop six inches off my legs. Then I'd get to go back to sea and have a few adventures. It's tough being stuck here stateside, on dry land. I looked around at the Shanghai Swabs. Most were merchant sailors. Some were from the battleships that had come into base for repairs—veteran petty officers with hash marks up and down their sleeves. I'd trade places with any one of them.

Seemed like the right thing to do—joining the Navy. I'd been working on tramp steamers for six years when the Japs bombed Pearl Harbor. I knew the Army would grab me in a flash, but hell, I didn't want to spend the war with my face in the mud. So I stepped up to enlist. Who would've guessed? Here I am with six times the sailing experience of your freshly-minted, wet-behind-the-ear ensign from Annapolis, but the Navy, in its infinite wisdom, decided I'd be more of an asset looking after drunks.

"Hey, Champ." The bartender caught my eye and grinned at me. "This one's on the house." He poured a shot from a bottle that looked like the good stuff he saved for himself. "That left hook of yours won me a pile of cash last month."

Seadog turned and looked me up and down with renewed interest.

I thanked the bartender for the drink and threw it back in one gulp, as expected. "So, you go to the exhibitions?"

"Every chance I get," the bartender replied. He turned to Seadog and poked his thumb at me. "You should see this guy's left-right combination. Where did you learn to punch like that, Champ?"

I picked up the beer that Joey had already ordered for me and took a swig before answering. "I was shipmates with a Brit, an ex-middleweight. Name was Colin—never did learn his last name. Met him on a freighter about seven years ago, when I was about sixteen. For some reason, he took me under his wing and taught me the basics. You pick up a lot of survival skills working on tramps."

"Ha!" Seadog joined the conversation. "I'll tell ya about survival." He proceeded to spin a yarn about escaping from cannibals in the South Pacific, and we whittled away the night, trying to top each other with tales of terror on the high seas. Every now and then, I'd look over and check on what kind of adventures Joey was having. He was seated at a scarred wooden table with two gals hanging on his every word.

I also noticed the four guys at one of the pool tables throwing ugly looks in Joey's direction. One, in particular, had cords in his bull neck thick as anchor chains. He didn't seem to take too kindly to Joey's talent for making the gals laugh.

By two bells, the bar crowd had thinned out, but Seadog was getting his second wind and launching into another tall tale.

A girl screamed.

I turned and saw Anchor Chain and one of his buddies going for Joey. Anchor was holding his cue stick like a baseball bat and the other guy had pulled out a switchblade.

"Watch it!" I shouted. But Joey had already seen them and was on his feet, reaching for a chair.

I grabbed two glass beer mugs off the bar and threw straight at their heads, forcing the swabs to cover up.

Joey smashed his chair against a third guy who'd decided to join the party. I charged into Anchor, landed my left-right combination, and relieved him of his cue stick. Using the butt of the stick, I smashed the second guy upside the head and stabbed the point up Anchor's nose. Blood spurted and he yelled in pain. Joey pummeled the fourth thug with the guy's own blackjack. The fella was out cold on the floor, but Joey kept pounding him. I could tell by the crazed look in Joey's eyes he'd crossed the line and was attacking for the pure pleasure of it. I dropped my stick and wrapped my arms around Joey in order to keep him from killing the bastard. He almost attacked me, but I bear hugged him until he finally calmed down. "Okay. Okay," Joey said.

"Get the fuck outta here!" The bartender yelled. "That means you, too, Champ!"

THE NEXT MORNING, the Captain chewed out Joey and me for breakfast. One of our "victims" had called the cops, wanting to press charges against us. The fella got Joey's name from one of the gals. And there's only one six-foot-four-inch sailor in San Diego. Me.

I figured we'd be thrown into the brig right then and there because of that free-for-all. With every lash of Captain's tongue, I mentally added another day to my sentence. His speech basically boiled down to, "What the hell were you two thinking?"

This is it, I thought. He's gonna take my stripes for sure.

Instead, the Captain ended with, "The police tell me the bartender doesn't remember any fight. Mister Cavanaugh, Mister Jules—you've already got furlough. Just get out of town. I don't want to see either of your mugs on this base for the next ten days."

Shocked, Joey and I stammered out our thank-yous. We saluted and got the hell out of there before Captain changed his mind.

Back at the barrack, I stood outside, smoked my pipe and wondered what to do next.

Joey said, "Well, you heard Captain's orders. We gotta scram—get outta here. I'm packin' right now."

I didn't move. That gift of ten days had saddled me

with a big problem. Going off base meant I needed money for food and lodging. On my own since the age of fifteen, I didn't have more cash than what was in my pocket. Besides, I figured the Navy's my home—where else was I gonna go?

I stood outside the barrack's door, puffing on my pipe. Through the doorway, I could see Joey shoving gear into the seabag on his bunk. Guess my lack of enthusiasm was pretty obvious. He stopped abruptly, turned to me, and said, "Hey, Nick. How about coming home to Kentucky with me and staying with my folks? You know we've got this casino just outside of Newport. Lots of chorus girls—" he wriggled his eyebrows like Groucho Marx, "—do a little screwing, a little gambling with the house's money. What d'ya say?"

I hesitated for a moment, then tapped out my pipe, walked in and started packing my bag.

Joey slapped me on my back. "Thattaboy! Then you can hop across the river into Cincinnati and go look up your own family. What's it been—eight years since you've seen them?"

"Cincinnati? Shit! I'd rather spend the next ten days in the brig."

3

SEPTEMBER 17

NEWPORT, KENTUCKY

"TAKE THE DAMN MONEY!"

Detective Steve Pope stared at the fifty dollars in the change tray on the table. He lifted his head up again and watched the waitress walk back to the bar. She added a teasing little wiggle to her hips, probably knowing his eyes were on her.

Pope looked back at the money.

"Don't be a stupid asshole, Steve. Take the goddamn money," Detective Virgil Ducker said again, with a little flick of his chin as through trying to push the greenbacks across the white tablecloth and closer to his cousin.

It was seven P.M. and Detectives Pope and Ducker had just ended their shift. They had walked the few short blocks from the police station to the Glenn Rendezvous for a quick drink in the supper club's bar before going home to their wives. Fifty dollars change for a five cent beer sure wasn't an honest mistake. Pope could almost see the strings attached to it.

Ducker prodded him again. "If we're gonna be partners, you gotta understand the rules. This is the way the game's been played for twenty years. Probably even longer."

Pope whispered back, "But it's more than I make in a week."

"We come in here almost every night. Think of it as Pete Schmidt's gift on account of your promotion."

Acid bubbled in Pope's stomach. Dammit, he should've been promoted to detective purely because he was good at his job—not because his benevolent uncle, Judge Ducker, decided to put in a good word for him with the chief of police.

Pope glanced over at the bar. Pete Schmidt, dressed in a white tuxedo, stood behind it. The casino owner smiled at him. As a patrolman, Pope had taken the occasional bribe of five or ten dollars—he knew if he didn't he'd be ostracized by the other cops. Everybody closed their fists around offered gifts. But one this size? Pope looked back at the change tray loaded with five tens. He knew if he took it, this was just the beginning. Didn't matter how high up you were, once you were on the payroll of the Cleveland Syndicate or independent casino operators like Pete Schmidt, Little Mexico had a way of pulling you down into the gutter real fast. She already had her arms around the mayor, the chief of police, and most of city council.

But he needed the money. Not that he was living the high life, feeding the slot machines or trying to make seven the hard way at any of the dozens of casinos surrounding city hall and the courthouse. The plain fact was cops were paid poorly because it was assumed they'd make it up on tips—not much different from their hip-swinging waitress.

Ducker leaned across the small table, bringing his face to within an inch of Pope's. "You and your sweet little lady have a baby on the way. Or have you figured out a way to eat air?"

"No!" Pope slammed the table with the palm of his hand, bouncing the tray of bills. "It's not right."

"Oh, c'mon, you're still that fresh-faced little altar boy. Grow up! You forget how hard it was to put food on the table a few years back?"

Pope felt like a hungry animal standing in front of a baited trap. He looked down at his hands, searching for an answer. His eyes rested on the frayed cuffs of his jacket. Even a cheap, off-the-rack replacement would cost half his week's salary.

Ducker's attention was drawn towards the entrance. "What does that guy want? Can't we have a drink in peace?"

Pope picked his head up and followed his cousin's gaze. A young patrolman had just entered the bar and was making his way towards them.

"Hate to disturb you," the patrolman said, when he reached their table. "Chief knew you two'd be having a drink here, so he sent me to get you. Wants both of you down at the river."

"Why?" Pope asked, thankful for the diversion.

Ducker wasn't so thankful. "What about Turnbull? He's on duty—saw him sign in just before we left the station."

"He went home sick," the patrolman answered. "Started throwing up all over the place."

"Oh, jeez. Again?" Ducker sighed. "All right, now what's happening down there?"

The patrolman leaned forward. "You know that barge that slammed into the Central Bridge, two o'clock this morning? Seems the divers they sent down are getting ready to haul up something more interesting than the load of steel girders that went overboard."

"Well, let's get going," Pope said. He jumped to his feet to follow the patrolman who had already started for the door.

Ducker's hand made a quick pass over the change tray. The fifty dollars disappeared. Before Pope could step away from the table, he felt his right wrist being gripped. A wad of crisp paper was shoved into the palm of his hand.

"Don't forget your change." Ducker smiled.

Pope hesitated—for a moment. He slipped the present into his pocket. Passing the bar on the way to the door, he glanced at the owner. Pete Schmidt raised a glass and winked.

Steve Pope felt the fingers of Little Mexico dig into his leg.

POPE AND DUCKER, in their own car, followed the patrolman around the barricades and parked under the bridge, which had been closed all day. Concerned there might be structural damage to the bridge itself, Kentucky state officials had called in engineers to inspect the piling.

The two detectives joined a huddle of uniformed men standing at the riverbank. Ducker, leading the way, called out, "What have we got?"

A Coast Guard lieutenant answered. "Divers found a body down there. We were waiting for you to arrive before we pulled him out. We'll take you out to the tug."

Pope, Ducker, and the Coast Guard lieutenant boarded a launch, a pimply-faced sailor at the helm. A few minutes later, aboard the tug, they stood in silence and stared down at the water. The metal chain clanked as the winch turned.

The Coast Guard lieutenant filled Ducker and Pope in on the salvaging activities of the day. He explained how, a half hour earlier, one of the divers had made the discovery while feeling around a steel girder on the river bottom, searching for a hooking point. "Seems he grabbed a handful of hair—with a head attached to it."

First to break the surface were two divers, one holding a metal lid. Then, with a whoosh of brown river water, they hauled out the drum itself. A human head was sticking out the open end. As the crane swung it over the deck, a couple of deck hands grabbed the metal barrel, steadied it, and turned it right side up. The crane set its catch on the deck.

Pope, Ducker, and the Coast Guard lieutenant circled the drum, making a cursory examination.

Ducker grunted. "Packed in cement. Must be mob— they don't go to that kinda trouble for anybody else."

Ducker leaned in close to study the victim's head, and scrunched up his face. "What the hell's he got in his mouth?"

Pope bent forward to take a look. "Cement."

"Yeah? Guess you're right. Now the next question. Is

33

this who I think it is?"

Pope nodded. "Yep. It's Charlie DePalma."

Ducker slapped Pope on the back. "It's Dandy Charlie all right. No wonder they gave you that promotion." The two straightened up.

Ducker took off his hat and held it in front of his balls as if paying respect to the dead body. "Dandy Charlie. There's already been a lot of scuttlebutt on the streets about where you suddenly disappeared to. I thought you had a much better sense of style than this," he said, shaking his head in mock sadness. "Never thought you'd be caught dead wearing a Newport nightgown."

———

BRUNO CARPELLA WAS at his spot in the Yorkshire Club, at the end of the bar where it curved at a right angle. The club was the major site of the Cleveland Syndicate's handbook activities. Now that Bruno had Dandy Charlie's collection job, he'd sit there for hours taking mental snapshots of everyone entering the club. He had a real good head for remembering faces, and knew this talent could be very helpful to his career.

The usual stream of ordinary, hardworking businessmen coming over the bridge from Cincinnati didn't interest Bruno. They always paid up. But when the door swung open and a tuxedoed gent strutted in with two flashy babes on his arms—that's when Bruno squinted and focused in. He'd learned one basic fact about guys in the dough: the more they flashed, the more they welshed. Bruno memorized every chin whisker on the guy's puss.

As Bruno pulled the cigar from his mouth, a bit of ash floated down and landed on the sleeve of his new suit. Bruno blew at the speck of ash—he didn't want to smear it into the expensive cream-colored wool. It sure was great being able to walk into Saul's Tailoring on Monmouth Street and plunk down cold hard cash for three or four handmade numbers— "Yessir, Mr. Carpella! Right away, Mr. Carpella!" At twenty-three years of age, Bruno was on his way.

Bruno felt good having Red Masterson's confidence, but too much of this could turn out to be a bad thing. He didn't want to be known as Red's Boy. "Bruno do this, Bruno do that." Not good for a guy with plans to climb to the top of the heap.

He knew he needed to establish his own turf away from Red. But show too much independence and Red was bound to realize Bruno could stab him in the back without batting an eye. He'd been chewing over how he was going to make his move without tipping his hand, when Red himself supplied the answer by suggesting Bruno set up shop at the Yorkshire Club. He jumped at the chance to mark his own territory away from Red's headquarters at the Merchant's Club.

The first night at the Yorkshire, Bruno had strutted around the club giving customers the once-over. He felt like one of those barons in an Errol Flynn movie who'd been given his own lands by King John as reward for faithful service. But halfway through the evening, the bartender cracked, "You're acting like a young pup who's been given a tree to piss on and making damn sure your scent's on every square inch of it. Stop annoying the customers."

Bruno had laughed it off, but he cut it out real fast.

Other than that minor gaff, things were sure going his way—Red had just given him another job.

Bruno took a big drag on his dollar cigar and squinted as the front door to the Yorkshire opened. It was Manny and Al. *'Bout fuckin' time they showed up.* "Where you guys been?" he said when they joined him at the bar.

Al smirked. "Lotta commotion down at the river."

Manny added, in his hoarse voice, "I think Dandy Charlie got run over by a barge."

"Yeah? So?" Bruno dismissed the old news with a flick of his cigar ash. "We got more important stuff to talk about." He looked around, making sure nobody was within hearing distance. "Red wants us to convince Carl Jules it would be a good business move for him to sell The Oasis."

Al scratched the back of his head, pushing his hat forward over his eyes. "That's way out there in the sticks."

"Yeah? So? He's making a lot of money out there in his classy joint and the boys in Cleveland don't like him competing with *their* fancy places. Don't forget, the Beverly Hills and Lookout House are out there in the sticks, too."

Al jabbed his thumb at the front entrance. "But what about the Levinson brothers right across the street in the Flamingo Club?"

"Don't you know nothin'? Come here. Manny, you too." The three hunched down together like they were huddled on a football field, working out their next play. "'Sleepout' Louie is allowed to operate because, even though him and his brothers are from Chicago, they're fronting for the Eastern Syndicate. So, it's kind of a courtesy that Cleveland is extending the boys in New York. Besides, they've got friends like Frank Costello and Trigger Mike Coppola—no one wants

36

to fuck with them. But Cleveland doesn't like independents like Carl Jules, Pete Schmidt over at the Glenn Rendezvous, or Buck Brady at the Primrose Club."

"Didn't Schmidt used to own the Beverly Hills a few years back?"

"Yeah, but Red got him to clear out and sell to Cleveland."

"Why'd they let him back into business over at the Rendezvous?" Al asked. "And what about Brady?"

"I don't know. They ain't our problems. Our job is to get Jules to sell out. That's all you need to know. And don't go blabbing to any of your drinking buddies, Al—just keep quiet like Manny here." Bruno waved a hand in Manny's direction. "I'm working out what to do next."

Just thinking of going after Carl Jules made Bruno so excited, he was having a tough time sitting on the bar stool and concentrating on the faces coming through the door. He'd sure like to visit Claudette for a quickie.

4

SEPTEMBER 18

THE OASIS WAS QUIET. All the gamblers, drinkers, and diners had had their fill and gone home. A slow night—no more than eighty customers. The front doors were shut on the last one at about 1:30 A.M.

By 2:00 A.M., the stage was cleared of band instruments, the dealers had accounted for all their chips, and the showgirls had hung up their feathered headdresses for the night. Carmelo Giuliani—or Carl Jules, as he was known to the locals—had even sent his head security man home early.

As Carl made his way around to the back of the bar, he

pulled his bow tie loose, and helped himself to a bottle of scotch. He welcomed the silence.

He poured himself a double, took a swallow, moved to the front of the bar, and sat on one of the stools. The letter in his tuxedo's breast pocket had been burning a hole in his chest all night. The cool, gracious exterior he'd shown his customers that evening lied about the rage that seethed in his veins.

Carl opened his jacket, slid his hand over the Beretta nestled in his shoulder holster, grabbed the offending letter and slammed it on the bar in front of him. He wasn't ready to go home yet. He needed this time alone.

Carl took another deep swallow of his drink and stared at the crumpled piece of paper. He'd only had time to read it through once, quickly, before the interruptions and distractions of running The Oasis demanded all his attention—even on a slow night. How was he going to break this rotten news to Pearl? He couldn't go home until he'd figured that out. Pearl was home sick with a fever tonight, but she'd never spent more than a day away from The Oasis and was bound to be back in the office tomorrow. He could pretend the letter never existed, but that wouldn't be the end of it. Next thing, there'd be a visitor from Cleveland. Then Pearl would really be pissed—at the situation *and* at him for not letting her in on it from the beginning. There had been times when he'd failed to tell her something he thought was insignificant and she'd flown into a rage. Not telling her this would definitely spark her fuse and have him fighting a war on two fronts.

Carl tasted bile in his throat. Another swallow of scotch failed to wash it back down.

"Fucking Lester! Thinks I'm gonna hand it all over to the Syndicate on a silver platter? Who the hell does he think he's dealing with?" Carl cuffed the letter and sent it flying down the length of the bar. That eased some of the pressure building up in his head, but punching the guy out would've been more satisfying.

Carl leaned forward, elbows on the bar, and stared into his scotch. He pulled absentmindedly on his thick, graying eyebrows. Carl looked up. The mirror at the back of the bar reflected someone moving behind him. He quickly swiveled around on the bar stool. "Ginnie?"

The showgirl was stepping away. "Um, sorry. I didn't mean to disturb you, Mr. Jules."

"What're you doing here?" Carl asked. He got off his stool, retrieved the letter, and stuffed it in his pocket. "Thought everyone had gone home."

Virginia Stevenson held up a gold cigarette lighter. "I was looking for Joey. He left this in the dressing room earlier this evening."

"The dressing room?" Carl cursed to himself. He didn't need this—not tonight. "Which one? The dancers'?"

"Um. Yeah," Ginnie answered, a slight shake in her voice.

Carl thrust out his hand. "I'll make sure he gets it."

Ginnie handed over the gold lighter, quickly stepped back, and turned to leave.

"Wait," Carl said, "I'm not ready to go yet, but I'll walk you to the back door and make sure you get into your car."

Ginnie gave him a polite smile.

She sure is pretty. Carl liked the sprinkling of freckles on her nose that she had tried to cover with makeup. The low lighting gave her flaming red hair a warmer glow. As they walked side by side out of the bar and through the darkened lobby, Carl appreciated the sensuality of her walk. He understood why his son had great difficulty keeping his hands off the dancers. Carl supposed he should go easy on Joey since he was home on leave, but those were the house rules for everybody, including himself.

As they walked past the sweeping staircase that led to the second floor offices, Carl heard a couple of groans. He knew immediately what was going on behind the closed door of the room the dealers used for their breaks. He glanced at Ginnie. She knew, too.

Carl marched to the door, grabbed the knob and pushed. It was locked. He pounded on the door and shouted, "Open up!"

Inside, there was a frantic, half-whispered exchange, some scuffling noises, and then footsteps. The door swung open.

"Hi, Dad," Joey said. He finished zipping up his fly, while the blond-haired chorus girl Carl had just hired two days ago tried to rearrange her ruffled feathers. Ginnie stared open-mouthed at the scene for a brief moment, spun on her heels, and ran into the gaming room. Carl could hear the *click click* of her heels on the polished floor, then the slam of the back door.

He pointed a finger at Joey's conquest. "You! Out!"

The blonde bent to pick up her shoes and, with eyes still downcast, sidled out of the room, squeezing between Carl and Joey. She made a dash for the dressing rooms.

Carl poked two fingers against Joey's chest, pushing him back into the room. "How many times have I told you? No fraternizing with the employees. Huh, Joey?"

Joey looked sheepish. He shrugged, flashed his "okay, you got me" look, and straightened the lapel of his tuxedo jacket.

Carl couldn't let this go by—not without some kind of slap on the wrist. "I mean it, Joey. Hands off. I can't keep discipline in this club and make exceptions for you."

Joey's eyes flashed angrily, and Carl could see a part of Pearl in them.

"What the hell you talking about, Dad? You can't tell me you've never fooled around with the dancers around here."

Carl held up a hand to protest. "That was—"

"Yeah, yeah, I know, 'a long time ago.' Guess you thought I was too young to understand what was going on. Well, I wasn't."

"That was then, this is now, and I'm telling you, don't fuck with the dancers. I got a lot of problems and I don't need any more just because my horny son's home on leave."

"Yeah, well, I'm a sailor and fucking is what sailors do on leave. All these babes and you tell me 'Hands off'? I—" Joey had a sudden thought and looked at his watch. "Shit, I'm late! Nick's train should be coming in any minute. See you later at home." He marched past Carl and slammed the door behind him, leaving Carl alone in the break room.

Carl ground his teeth and clenched and unclenched his fists. First, the damn letter from that wop's mouthpiece, now this from his own son. No respect from anyone. "God, what have I done to deserve this?" He needed another drink.

Carl opened the door and walked out into the lobby. It was empty. He walked into the Caravan Room—the main dining area—past the stage, to the dressing rooms. He searched the rooms. Nobody there. He wondered if the blonde had the guts to show up for work tomorrow. Carl hoped she did. He couldn't remember her name, but she was a good dancer, and in his book everybody deserved three strikes before getting kicked out.

Kicked out! That's exactly what Cleveland wanted to do to him and his family. Carl shut the door to the last dressing room and went back to the bar to finish the scotch he'd left there. He took a couple of swallows of his drink, pulled out the letter and unfolded it.

He read the name on the letterhead. "Charles E. Lester, Attorney-at-Law." His grip tightened on the letter. "Two-bit lawyer." He read the amount offered, "$100,000," and spat at it. "There! That's my answer."

It had taken Carl ten long years of sweat and blood to build The Oasis. He'd done a damn good job. Just as swanky a place as Pete Schmidt's Beverly Hills Country Club. Not bad for the son of a mining town barber. Cleveland thinks they can come down here, say "we want it" and, bang, it's theirs? Those guys better think again. Maybe he was too stubborn or just stupid, but this was the Jules' place and he and Pearl weren't about to let some big organization push them out for any amount. Not like Schmidt, who got shafted out of his Beverly Hills. And they sure as hell weren't going to sell out like Jimmy Brink did, handing over his Lookout House for a piddling ten percent of the take—even if that deal also included ten percent of the Beverly Hills.

"This place is mine!" Carl's shout echoed throughout the empty Oasis. His right fist tightened around his glass of scotch. He slammed it down on the edge of the bar's porcelain sink, shattering the glass into pieces. He opened his hand to find a deep cut in his palm. Blood started trickling down his

43

wrist. "Fuck," he said, as he felt the sting of the alcohol. Carl reached into his pocket, pulled out a handkerchief, and wrapped it around his cut hand. Time to go home.

He picked the pieces of broken glass out of the sink, and threw them in the garbage, then bent down and retrieved the spit-stained letter from off the floor and stuffed it into his jacket's inner pocket. After turning off some of the overhead lights, he left the bar, crossed the lobby, and trudged wearily up the stairs to his office.

Carl opened the brand new Wells Fargo safe he'd had built into one wall of his office, took out the day's profits, and awkwardly flicked through the stack of bills with his left hand. Yep, it was all there. He took a leather pouch out of the safe, put the money in it, and slid the pouch into the left side pocket of his jacket.

Blood soaked through the white linen handkerchief. Carl thought about changing to a fresh bandage, but decided not to bother—it was only a ten minute drive to his home in Fort Thomas.

He put on his snap-brim hat, automatically giving it a rakish tilt, and hurried down the stairs, and into the gaming room. He turned off the light in the money cage and made his way to the back exit, hitting switches that doused the lights over the crap tables.

At the door, Carl stopped and took out a pack of cigarettes, shook one free, and put it between his lips. He reached into his pants pocket and pulled out Joey's lighter. "Hmm, he'll be wondering where he left that."

Carl lit his cigarette, slipped the lighter back into his pocket, and pulled open the door. It was like stepping into the flight path of a swarm of angry bees. He was hit again and again in rapid succession. The first bullet got him in the left shoulder, taking his breath away and spinning him off balance. The second missed. The third hit him in the spine, as he tried to catch his breath. The fourth touched off an enormous explosion of pain in his head.

Carl did not hear the fifth, sixth, and seventh gunshots.

———

Pearl woke with a start. At first she thought it must have been the front door slamming—Carl coming home from The Oasis. She sat up in bed and listened. Silence. She looked at the clock on the bedside table—2:45 A.M. Guess they were having a good night. Even so, Carl was sure to be home soon.

Pearl figured she looked like hell after spending most of the day in bed and didn't want Carl to see her that way, so she went to the bathroom and splashed her face with cold water. She still felt a little wobbly as she made her way back to the bedroom. She picked up one of the tubes of lipstick on her vanity, colored her lips with her favorite shade—military red—and ran a comb through her gold curls. She put on a blue silk robe, stepped into a pair of black velvet mules, and padded downstairs to the kitchen.

It was their usual routine to have something to eat when they got home from the club. Pearl set out some dishes on the kitchen table, and pulled a plate of fried chicken out of the icebox. There was enough chicken for Joey and his friend Nick, too. When they finally got here, she thought. Why weren't *they* home yet? Joey had said his friend's train was arriving at midnight.

45

She looked at the kitchen clock—3:10.

Pearl walked out to the living room, picked up a copy of *The Saturday Evening Post* from the coffee table and settled into her chair by the fireplace. After a few minutes of flipping pages, she realized she wasn't looking at what was on them. It was unusual for her to be at home waiting for Carl—it made her restless and uneasy. She threw the magazine back down on the table, walked first to the front window and glanced out, then went to the kitchen, stood in the doorway, and stared at the plate of fried chicken in the center of the table. She guessed she was over her flu or whatever it was that had kept her in bed all day, because, suddenly, she felt very hungry. Maybe she'd give The Oasis a call to find out when Carl was coming home. She went to the phone on the table by the staircase, picked up the receiver, and dialed Carl's office. It rang five or six times. He's probably downstairs, she thought, and dialed The Oasis' main telephone number and let that ring eight times. Must have just missed them, she thought. Carl was probably on his way and would be home in ten minutes. Pearl started slicing some bread.

Ten minutes passed.

Then fifteen.

Pearl paced from the kitchen to the living room, looking out the window, looking at the telephone. Where the hell is he? She picked up the phone and dialed the home number of their head security man. It was picked up on the third ring.

A gruff male voice said, "William's residence. This better be an emergency."

"Hunch? It's Pearl. Do you know where Carl is? I've called the club and nobody answers."

There was silence on Hunch's end—but only for a moment. "What time is it? Three-thirty? I'll drive back there and check on things."

Hunch's voice had a forced calmness. Something was wrong. Pearl felt a twinge of anxiety. "Come pick me up first—I'm going with you."

"Well, I—"

"Who signs your checks, Hunch?" Pearl's voice was firm.

"Okay, okay. See you in ten minutes."

"Good." Pearl cradled the phone and ran upstairs to throw on some clothes and pack her chrome-plated .22 automatic in her purse.

5

LOGBOOK ENTRY: 0130 Hours

"WANNA PLAY A HAND, SAILOR?" The wrinkled gent sitting across from me fanned a deck of cards. He'd seen me put down my dog-eared Armed Services Edition of *THE BIG SLEEP*, and probably figured it was a signal that I was ready for something else to do.

I smiled back at the old cardsharp and shook my head. "Sorry, I'm kinda bushed."

He shrugged and dealt himself a game of solitaire.

I looked around at the other passengers with whom I'd shared the railcar for the past three days. They'd been an easy lot to get along with, even when the train was stuck for five hours in the middle of Missouri, while they cleared a derailment up the track ahead of us. The engineer had been trying to make up time, but we were still two and a half hours behind schedule and Cincinnati was an hour away.

Joey's dad had wired him money to take a plane in from San Diego. When Joey offered to buy me a ticket to fly along, I said, "No, thanks." The thought of all those takeoffs and landings didn't appeal to me. I wasn't in a rush, and I like seeing the countryside. In fact, I wouldn't mind if the train rolled on past Cincinnati, shot across the Atlantic Ocean, right between the Pillars of Hercules, and smacked into Italy's boot—Salerno, to be exact. Hell, that's probably the only way I'd get into some actual fighting in this war.

I peered through my reflection in the window to see if there was anything out there. The Indiana countryside zipped by, black and empty.

The rhythmic clatter of metal wheels on track and the side to side rocking of the railroad car must have put me to sleep. Next thing I knew, I was standing in a huge boxing ring, dressed in fighting trunks, my boxing gloves laced up good and tight.

The tuxedoed announcer at the mike pointed to me and said, "And in this corner, standing at six foot four and weighing in at two hundred and five pounds—the pride of the U.S. Navy—Petty officer third class Nick Cavanaugh!"

Cheers filled the air. I looked around and saw millions of sailors dressed in summer whites standing in a sea of black like stars in the moonless Indiana sky. Above me, a giant Old Glory hung from invisible rafters. In the corner opposite me, stood my opponent. He was a few inches shorter and a good twenty pounds heavier, but I couldn't make out his face.

A bell rang. Immediately, we circled each other. Even at close quarters, his face was out of focus, but the arrogant thrust of his chin—like he was daring me to throw the first punch—was familiar. I did. A solid left jab to his cheek. The impact snapped his head back and his features into focus.

"Dad?"

He smiled at me with a crooked grin and said, "That's your best, Nicky boy?"

I smashed him a good one, this time opening a cut over his right eye.

"You forgot to put your full weight into that one," Dad said, in that belittling tone he always used with me. Never good enough.

I threw a quick three-punch combination to his head, breaking through his guard and scoring each time. "How's that?" I asked.

The crowd of sailors roared, drowning out Dad's voice, but I read the answer in his smirk. Still not good enough.

We circled each other, Dad throwing punches that never reached me. I kept pounding him, until blood covered my gloves. Dad's eyes were almost swollen shut, but I couldn't knock the sneer off his face. Now each time I landed a shot to his head, the power of my punch tore away a strip of flesh, exposing bone. Each strip of flesh that flew into the crowd was greeted by a cheer. I'd had enough of this, but my arms wouldn't obey me—it was as if they had minds of their own.

The crowd surged forward into the ring, chanting, "Sailor! Sailor! Sailor!"

Someone grabbed my shoulder. "Hey, sailor!"

I felt the cool hardness of glass against my temple and opened my eyes.

"Sailor!" The old cardsharp's face was inches away from mine. "Your stop's comin' up."

I lifted my head and rubbed the side that had been pressed against the window. A conductor walked down the aisle, singing, "*Uuun*-ion Terminal....*Cinnn*-cinn*aaatah*."

I looked out the window. It was still black out there. Cincinnati's Union Terminal was on the western edge of the city, so I wasn't expecting to see the downtown lights. But that kind of fit—Cincinnati was always dark to me.

Not everyone was getting off. I looked around at the passengers who were still in their seats, sleeping, and wondered what dark thoughts invaded *their* dreams.

I stood up and got my seabag from the overhead ledge, and stowed my Raymond Chandler book in it. "Hope things work out for you in Baltimore," I said to the old gent. "Thanks for the card games."

He saluted. "And good luck to you, sailor."

A few minutes later, the train pulled into the station. I got off and walked across the marbled floor of the Terminal's waiting room. The last time I'd walked there was eight years earlier with a ticket clutched in my fifteen year old hand, hoping nobody I knew would come up and try to stop me from escaping.

Now, here I was, walking down these marbled corridors again, hoping nobody would see me coming back. Because I wasn't coming back. I sure hoped Joey was at the information booth like we'd planned. With the train being so late, there was a chance he wouldn't be. No, hell, he'd find out when the train was arriving and be there.

With all the trains coming and going even at 0230 hours, there were lots of people milling around. Everybody stared at me. Some even smiled as they passed by, and I wondered, "Do they know me?" After it happened so many times with nobody stopping and saying, "Hey, Nick! How you doin'?" I realized it was probably my uniform. And maybe my height had something to do with it, too.

I entered the main concourse and stopped to admire the domed ceiling over one hundred feet above me. Painted in shades of yellow and orange, it seemed to glow. Reaching up to that dome, bright mosaic murals on the walls showed scenes of men and women working hard at their jobs: early settlers, soldiers, soap makers, meat packers, riverboat men—there were more than a dozen giant murals, all around the concourse. It was kind of overwhelming to realize they were created with pieces of colored ceramic smaller than a nickel.

I headed over to the large information booth in the center of the concourse and walked around it. Joey wasn't there. Maybe he was late—that'd be just like him. I paced up and down a couple of times, then decided to go stand outside in front.

From the top step, I looked down the length of the plaza—a stretch of lawns and fountains pointing towards the lit skyline of Cincinnati's downtown. Just a few blocks away was where I'd spent the first part of my life. I wondered if Dad and Mom were still slaving away in that greasy kitchen of his stinking chili parlor. My little brother Jimmy'd be thirteen by now—maybe planning his own escape.

I pulled out my pipe and tobacco, filled up, and settled in on my watch.

A long driveway came up one side of the plaza, curved around in front of the terminal's entrance and went back down the other side of the plaza, out to the road. For ten minutes, I stood watching the cars drive up and drop off or pick up passengers. There was lots of hugging and kissing and hauling baggage. It was entertaining. For a while.

But then I saw the black Cadillac. A real beauty—shining and new. Well, as new as they got. With this war going on, only a lucky few had 1942 model cars. But a '42 *Cadillac?* Well, you had to be lucky *and* rolling in dough to be driving one of those.

The lucky bastard stopped right in front of me, leaned over and yelled out the opened window on the passenger side, "How ya doin, Nick?"

"Joey?"

He shut off the engine, got out from the driver's side, and ran around to me. We greeted each other with a couple of light punches to the chest. My fist made contact with something hard just below Joey's armpit.

"What'cha got there?" I asked.

Joey opened the jacket of his tux and flashed the Beretta he was carrying in a shoulder holster. "Feels good to be fully dressed," he said, patting the gun. "And you gotta be dressed in Newport."

6

PEARL SAT NEXT to Hunch in silence as he drove to The
Oasis. The car sped through the darkness, rolling up and down
the road that cut across the hills between Route 27 and Route
9 where the casino was located. Not once did they see lights
from another car. They turned up the drive. To Pearl, the Oasis
never looked more isolated than it did at that moment.

Hunch wheeled into the parking lot and as soon as
Pearl saw the back door ajar, she knew something was terribly
wrong.

"Oh my God," Pearl cried, as she pushed on the

passenger side door.

Hunch yelled at her, "Wait." He stamped on the brake pedal and, as the car skidded to a halt, Pearl jumped out and ran.

"Carl! Oh, Lord, it's Carl!" Pearl's screams bounced off the stucco building.

Whipping out his gun, Hunch sprinted to the doorway where Pearl was already kneeling beside Carl's body. The hem of her dress soaked up some of the blood that had pooled around him.

"Honey, say something. *Please!*"

Hunch said, "Don't move him."

"I know, I know." Pearl carefully checked for a pulse on Carl's neck. "He's still alive. Call Doc—no, wait. What am I thinking? This is too much for him to handle. We're going to have to call an ambulance."

"That'll mean the cops get involved."

"I don't care—we'll deal with that later. Now go. Use the phone in the money cage."

Gun at the ready, Hunch cautiously stepped over Carl and disappeared into the gaming room.

Pearl knew that within minutes of Hunch placing the call, she'd have to deal with more than just the ambulance attendants. Right behind them would be the cops, a couple of detectives and, right on their heels, a handful of newspaper photographers. Without moving Carl, she felt the side pockets of his jacket and pulled out the money pouch, then lifted the front of his jacket by the lapel and slid his gun out of its holster. At the same time, she noticed a badly creased piece of paper in his breast pocket and took that, too. She glanced at the letterhead, recognized the name, and stuffed it into her purse to read later.

Hunch poked his head out the door. "They're on the way—I called Doc, too. I'm just gonna do a quick search inside."

"Wait," Pearl said, holding out the gun and money pouch, "take these. We'll never get them back if they're found on Carl."

Hunch stuffed the gun and money in his pockets and went back inside.

Pearl turned to Carl and gently stroked the side of his head that hadn't been bloodied. She patted his dark curls, then bent close to his ear and whispered, "You damn well better not die on me, Carmelo Giuliani."

———

LOGBOOK ENTRY: 0345 Hours

"WHERE'D YOU STEAL this baby from?" I asked Joey, as I stroked the soft leather of the front seat.

Joey cocked his eyebrow and grinned. "Ritzy, huh?" He pulled away from the train station and steered the Cadillac down the drive out into the street. "I'd like to say it's mine, but it ain't. It's my Pop's. Some big wig was late in paying off his IOU, so this hot little number got thrown in as interest."

"Nice." I answered in such a clipped, automatic way, it might have sounded like I didn't really mean it. At that moment, we were skirting the west end of my old neighborhood, and I was staring out the window, perturbed.

I wasn't prepared for the way I felt seeing it again—thought I'd completely severed all ties to the place. We turned a corner and passed by Old Man Schuler's drugstore where I used to hang out—me and a bunch of other twelve-year-olds looking for trouble. I remembered the day I beat up that bully, and smiled....Well, I guess this place still had a hold on me. But, at the same time, I wanted to tell Joey to step on it and get me the hell out of there.

Joey broke the silence. "Guess you're pretty tired. Sorry I'm late picking you up."

"Yeah, for a minute there, I figured you were probably having such a good time screwing around, you forgot to come and get me."

Joey laughed. "So I was. But it was a fight with my Pop that really made me late."

"And then he tossed you the keys to the Cadillac?"

"He didn't have to—he keeps the keys in the ignition." Joey stayed focused on the road ahead as we approached the L & N Bridge. "You should see the rust bucket I've had to drive the past few days. I wanted to give you a classier ride, so I just took it."

Halfway across the bridge, Joey pointed out the windshield. "They fished a body outta the water over there at the Central Bridge a few hours ago. Some poor bastard packed in cement."

"Friend of yours?"

Joey laughed. "Don't know yet. But probably someone Pop knows."

On the Kentucky side, we turned onto what looked like one of Newport's main streets. It was lit up and open for business. As we drove down the one-way street, I noticed all the parking spaces were filled and there were people going in and out of the bars even at that hour.

"This is York Street," Joey announced. "There're some

hot spots here we can come back to some other night."

Seemed like there were two or three clubs on every block. Some were holes-in-the-wall. Others looked like they had money behind them and shouted out their names in big neon letters—YORKSHIRE CLUB, FLAMINGO.

We turned left on Tenth and, as we cut across the next main street, Joey jerked his thumb out the window. "This is Monmouth Street. Lots of action here, too. Up the next block, there's a gal I want you to meet—a real honey. She's got special talents—knows exactly what a guy wants the very second he thinks it. You'd swear she was right inside your head, reading your mind. You'll like Claudette."

The rest of the drive took us through darkened residential streets, with each neighborhood looking a little less seedy than the one before it until, suddenly, I realized the houses were pretty damn respectable, almost Andy Hardyish. It was like being in the middle of a Hollywood studio's idea of life in the Midwest. The homes came with big trees, well-tended lawns, and wraparound porches—all part of the American Dream. Hell, I could almost smell the apple pie. So this was Fort Thomas. No wonder they processed so many GIs here. Before shipping out to their various units, those green recruits sure got an eyeful of what they were fighting for.

Joey turned into the driveway of one of those Andy Hardy homes and said, "Here we are."

"Wow! Impressive! First the car, now this house—your folks are pretty well set, aren't they?"

Joey shrugged. "They do okay." He grabbed my bag from the trunk, and I followed him up the walkway, onto the porch. He held the door open for me to go in first, then closed it gently behind him and said, "Gotta be quiet. My mom's

58

probably sleeping—she wasn't feeling too good today."

He motioned with his head for me to follow him up the oak staircase. At the top of the stairs, he came to an abrupt halt and stared ahead to the open door at the end of the hallway. Beyond it, I could see a white four-poster bed. Joey dropped my bag, walked down the hallway and poked his head in the room. "Mom?"

He turned and said to me over his shoulder, "She's not in bed." He tried another room, pushing open the door, and calling out, "Mom? You in here?"

The look on his face told me things weren't right, and I watched, feeling a little useless, as he made a quick search of the rooms on that floor.

"She's not here," Joey said, a worried look on his face.

"Maybe she went to the casino?"

"No, Pop was closing up. Besides, she didn't have a car." Joey pushed past me and ran down the stairs. "I'm calling the club."

I followed him down and sat on the bottom step, staying out of his way. Joey hurried through the rooms on the main floor, shouting "Mom?" He came back to where I was sitting, picked up the phone on a small table by the staircase and dialed a number. His eyes darted nervously as he listened to it ring on the other end. He broke the connection and dialed a second number. Waited. Broke that connection, and dialed a third number.

A moment later, Joey said, "Mrs. Williams? This is Joey Jules. Sorry to wake you. Is Hunch—what?" He listened. "Oh, shit." He slammed the receiver down and punched the wall. "That fucking Cleveland crowd!"

———

PEARL SAT IN the smoke-filled waiting room, her daughter Lauretta at her side. Hunch and Doc Miller paced up and down in front of them, puffing nervously on their cigarettes. Nobody spoke.

The hospital staff had rushed Carl into surgery, and it was obvious to Pearl, by the way they moved and barked out orders to each other, that her husband was hanging onto life just by his fingertips.

Lauretta reached over and gently massaged her mother's shoulder. Pearl smiled back at her, thankful that Doc had thought to pick her up on the way to the hospital. She wished she knew where Joey was.

Pearl wondered if riding beside Carl in the ambulance would be the last time she'd see him alive. She wished he'd been able to speak to her. All the way to the hospital, Pearl had spoken softly in his ear, telling him how much she loved him and needed him. "Hold on, Carl," she'd said. "You've got to make it." What if he didn't? She'd have to keep things going by herself.

Pearl stroked the brim of Carl's hat, which she held on her lap, and stared straight ahead, fighting back her tears. Clutching the gold crucifix around her neck, she tapped it against her chest, and prayed silently. *Oh, God, please forgive me. I'm so sorry, Carl. It's all my fault.*

———

RAYMOND TWITTY ENTERED the square brick building and climbed the stairs to his second floor apartment. It had been a slow night at The Oasis. The band had been let go earlier than usual, so he'd gone looking for a card game.

Raymond switched the saxophone case from his right hand to his left, pulled out the keys from his pocket and unlocked the door. Inside, he threw the case on the frayed brown sofa, took off his tuxedo jacket, and hung it on the back of a wooden chair. In the tiny kitchenette, he yanked open the door of the ice box and grabbed a beer.

"I shouldn't have asked for that third card," he said to nobody. Now he was out a half week's salary. He cracked the top off the bottle on an opener attached to the edge of the counter, and took a swig. Nobody to blame but himself.

Raymond wiped his hand across his forehead, plastering down his wispy, sweat-drenched hair. The air inside the boxy one-room apartment was stifling. He went over to the window and tried to yank it open. His 4-F arms strained with the effort when it got stuck halfway up. Raymond cursed loudly a few times, finally managing to get it completely open, then stood in front of it, stared out at the fire escape and breathed in. Two, three, four times. He went to the sofa, sat down, and placed his beer on the floor. He flicked open the clasps on his saxophone case, and pulled out a snapshot.

"Pearl," he whispered.

She smiled back at him, leaning forward, arms on the bar. Her large white breasts spilled out the top of a low-cut gown.

Raymond began caressing the black and white photograph. His fingers stroked down her neck, along the line of her cleavage, and over the curve of her breasts. He closed his eyes, saw it in Technicolor, and went hard.

7

LOGBOOK ENTRY: 0400 Hours

ON THE WAY TO THE HOSPITAL, Joey told me his father had been shot. He seemed convinced the Cleveland Syndicate was responsible, and briefly filled me in on the territorial battles taking place in Newport. He was silent the rest of the ride, but I could tell from the set of his jaw and the way he white-knuckled the steering wheel, Joey was trying to keep his temper in check.

Shit. What a way to start a leave. I decided to keep my mouth shut and just watch and listen, figuring I was in for a pretty interesting time.

At the hospital, we didn't need any help finding Joey's mother. The waiting room was right there at the entrance and as soon as we walked in, she called out to Joey, got up out of her chair, and gave him a big hug.

Joey's mom was a knockout—blond curls, full red lips. Her blue dress was kind of plain, except for the brownish splotch on its hem and the way she filled out the top. I stared down at two mounds of soft flesh, a crucifix nestled in between. The delicate gold medal flashed the order: *Eyes front, mister! No peeking!* Catching myself, I turned away, and stepped back to give them privacy. I felt like an intruder.

A younger, thinner version of her was seated in a red leather chair against the wall. I didn't know Joey had a sister, but I guessed that's who she was.

Joey asked his mom what was happening. She said she didn't know anything, and all they could do was wait and pray.

I was still looking at the younger woman in the chair when Joey said, "Ma. This is my pal, Nick Cavanaugh."

I quickly turned and took off my rig. My attraction to her made me kind of nervous and when she looked at me with round blue eyes, my hands busied themselves, rolling up my cap. "Pleased to meet you, Mrs. Jules."

She extended her hand. She was a pretty little thing, soft and feminine on the outside, but when she shook my hand, I felt the grip of a person who'd take shit from nobody.

"Call me Pearl," she said.

I nodded. "Pearl." And let go of her hand.

Joey indicated the young woman in the chair. "This is my big sister, Lauretta." We nodded to each other, and then Joey led me over to the two men who'd been hanging back a bit like I was. They seemed to belong, but looked more like bodyguards than family.

Like most fellas I run into, these two gorillas pulled themselves up as far as their spines would go and puffed out their chests before shaking my hand.

I looked eye-to-eye with the grim, muscle-bound guy, introduced to me as Hunch Williams. Joey said, "Hunch is an old pal of Dad's. He's in charge of our security."

The other man was middle-aged, wore steel-rimmed glasses, was a good six inches shorter than me, about Joey's height, and very fit. He smiled when he shook my hand. "Hi. I'm Doc Miller."

"You the family doctor?"

One corner of his mouth twitched in a quick smile. "Well, I sometimes do patch people up. But usually, I'm the band leader."

"Joey!" The tone of Pearl's voice commanded everyone's attention. "What happened tonight?"

"How the fuck should I know?"

"Don't use that language when you talk to me. What time did you leave the club?"

"Around two."

Hunch aimed his grim look at Joey and said, "I thought the club was empty when Carl sent me home."

"Yeah, well I was just talking to one of the girls."

Pearl glared at her son. "What happened after you *talked* to the girl?"

"I went to pick up Nick."

"You took the Cadillac?"

Joey shrugged. "Yeah."

"With your father's permission?"

Another little shrug. "Yeah."

Joey was lying. I wondered why.

Pearl said, "That's real hard to believe, Joey. Your father complains bitterly about the gas rationing and how he can't get by with just a book of A stamps for the Cadillac, but he lets you drive it into Cincinnati? It's—" she looked down at the floor and pinched the bridge of her nose. "What was your dad doing when you left?"

"I don't know. He was having a drink, I guess."

"Having a drink *alone?*" Pearl shook her head. "That's not like him." She paused for a moment. "The only time Carl stays by himself is when he's got a big problem."

Pearl snapped a look at where she'd been sitting, then quickly marched over and picked up a purse. She rummaged around inside it, pulled out a creased piece of paper and read it. I could hear her whisper the word "shit".

"What?" Joey said, moving quickly to his mother's side. Hanging over her shoulder, he read the document she held out in front of her. He turned and kicked a chair halfway across the waiting room.

"Joey!" Pearl snapped at him. "Don't you go out there waving your gun around. We don't know who did it."

"Oh, c'mon. Don't tell me—"

"No. They're not going to send a letter, then gun him down before we've had a chance to answer."

Joey cocked his head and squinted at her. "Why not? They figure Dad's not going to sell, so they get him out of the way then start pressuring you."

Pearl seemed to retreat into her own thoughts. She sat down, pulled a cigarette out of her purse, and lit up. Obviously, that was the end of the conversation. Each of us retreated into our own world and hunkered down for a watch.

No one stopped to tell me what the letter was about—not that I expected them to. But I guessed it had something to do with the Cleveland Syndicate wanting to squeeze Joey's parents out of their business. I couldn't tell who made more sense—Joey or Pearl. This was a new world to me and I didn't know what rules they lived by. Or if they made them up as they went along.

A COUPLE OF hours later, a doctor came into the waiting room and called Pearl over. Joey and Lauretta jumped up from their seats and hurried over to hear what he had to say. It didn't look great. Their faces remained grave as the doctor explained Carl Jules' condition.

The doctor left. As Pearl turned and walked to where Hunch and Doc waited, Lauretta burst into tears. Joey put his arm around his sister to comfort her. Even though I was standing a few feet away from Hunch and Doc, I heard Pearl's sobering announcement to them.

"Carl's alive, but he's still unconscious. The doctors aren't worried about the injury to his shoulder. It's the shots he took in the head and back that have done the most damage." Pearl took a deep breath. "They don't know if Carl will ever come out of it. And even if he does, they don't know if he will ever walk again." She paused, looked down at the floor, then spat out, "Nobody knows nothin'."

———

"PEARLIE? ARE YOU THERE? Where am I? What's happening?" Darkness surrounded Carl and he was shouting as loudly as he could, but the shouts echoed only in his head. No sound came out of his mouth.

Even if he could make a sound, who would hear it? He was alone, floating in a black sky.

It was cold. He felt it seeping in through the tips of his fingers and toes. Carl began shivering uncontrollably as icy liquid coursed through his veins and filled his heart with dread. Suddenly, he was falling.

"Pearlie!" he shouted in his head once again.

An angry voice responded, but it was unintelligible.

Carl looked around, trying to locate it. The voice sounded like it was coming up out of a well, and he realized he was falling through the blackness towards it.

A face appeared out of the void.

"Joey!"

His son, cursing through clenched teeth, opened his mouth and Carl plunged through, continuing down into the void, away from Joey's rage.

A white speck in the blackness caught his eye. It grew larger as he fell towards it. It fluttered. A bird? No, a piece of paper. Carl reached out and grabbed at it. He brought it close and read: *Charles E. Lester, Attorney-At-Law.*

He tried to throw the letter away, but it flew back, and wrapped itself around his head, covering his face, trying to suffocate him. Carl struggled to free himself, tearing away handfuls of paper. He felt the shreds of paper harden into metal, and hurled them into the void.

He was almost free when the pieces of metal shot back from the darkness, slamming into his shoulder, his back, his head. The black void turned blood red.

8

STEVE POPE SLID behind the wheel of his car and yawned. He'd had a sleepless night. Here it was already 7:30 in the morning, time to start his regular shift. It felt like he'd just crawled home an hour ago. By the time he and Ducker had finished with Dandy Charlie—dropping him off at the morgue and writing up their reports—it was two A.M. Pope didn't get to bed until after three.

But it wasn't just the sight of Dandy Charlie's head sticking out of a bucket of cement that kept Pope awake. The fact he'd accepted Pete Schmidt's "gift" also kept him tossing and turning for those scant few hours.

Pope turned the key in the ignition, shifted into gear, and pulled away from the curb. He aimed the car in the direction of the police station.

Pope had to make a plan—this was only the beginning. There were sure to be more "gifts" coming his way and he didn't want to have to explain where all the extra cash came from to his wife. She'd be frightened if she knew what he was getting involved in. The whole thing made him nervous, too.

Pope had decided, while shaving that morning, to open a safe deposit box and carry the key on him all the time. His wife would never know, since the family finances were his department. He also decided to go to confession that Saturday.

Pope made a left turn off Monmouth onto Fourth Street, drove the block and a half to the police station and pulled into the parking area.

Ducker was waiting for him at the station desk, sipping at his cardboard container of coffee. "Hey, hey, buddy boy. Your wife make you sleep on the sofa? You look like shit." Then added, "Figured out how you're gonna spend your gift?"

Pope grunted and made a beeline for the box of sinkers and coffee the deli down the street had delivered.

Ducker smiled and, ignoring his cousin's less than sunny disposition, followed him and kept right on yapping. "Think they've got a road crew over at the morgue trying to crack open Dandy Charlie with their jackhammers."

"That'll work," Pope answered, his mouth full of donut. He wasn't in the mood for Ducker and wondered how long this new partnership was going to last. Ducker's cavalier attitude towards the corruption and violent activities that

69

poisoned Newport was going to drive him crazy. On the other hand, Pope thought, his own Boy Scout attitude probably frustrated the hell out of ol' live-and-let-live Virg.

Pope signed in and headed towards his desk. Ducker, already working on his second coffee, tagged along behind him. They were halfway down the hall, when Acting Chief of Police George Gugel called out from his office. "Ducker! Pope! In here!"

The two detectives shuffled into Gugel's lair and waited for him to finish playing with some papers on his desk. Pope let his eyes wander around the office, taking in the rows of citations and pictures of Gugel smiling and shaking hands with local big wigs.

Gugel finally dotted the *i* and crossed the *t* of whatever note he was writing to himself. "Okay, boys. Had a shooting early this morning around two-three o'clock over at The Oasis —Carl Jules. The county sheriff asked for our help."

Ducker whistled.

"Yeah. Jules is lying unconscious over there in the hospital. Can't talk, no witnesses."

Pope asked, "Who found him?"

"Mrs. Jules and his head of security, Hunch Williams."

Ducker muttered, "Now there's a guy who knows how to do his job."

Gugel let that pass. "She said he was late coming home from the club, so she called Mr. Williams and they went to investigate. All we got are a couple of bullets they dug out of him in surgery. We got the area cordoned off. Go see what you can find."

Pope said, "If we find anything relevant we'll send them to the FBI lab in Washington to check for fingerprints."

70

Gugel shrugged.

"I guess," Pope continued, "we should talk to the Jules family about any threats made—"

"Look," Gugel said, gathering up the papers on his desk. He slid them into a file folder, and handed it to Ducker. "I know you fellas are working on Charlie DePalma, but I'm giving you this case, too. They're two of a kind—just hoods knocking each other off."

Pope was opening his mouth to say something else when Ducker nudged him to stay quiet, and said, "Okay, Chief. We'll get on it."

"Good."

Ducker cued Pope it was time to leave with a quick jerk of his head toward the door.

Out in the hall, Pope asked, "What's with all the sign language?"

"C'mon," Ducker said. He led the way back to the squadroom, and sat down in his chair. "Listen, cuz." He hoisted his legs up onto the desk, and crossed his size eleven feet on top of the green, ink-stained blotter. "The Chief doesn't much care what the hoods in this town do to each other. He doesn't want to divert too much manpower from the good citizenry of Newport and waste it on hoods. So, he's given the cases to me, er, us because he's confident we'll give 'em the treatment they deserve."

Pope waited for his cuz to elaborate. After a long moment of silence, he finally understood. "Oh. I get it. We're supposed to bury them, right?"

Ducker nodded.

No, thought Pope, his jaw clenching. It was going against the grain, but he had to do his job.

Pope leaned close to Ducker and spoke in a low, forceful voice. "Just 'cause I took the money to turn a blind eye to the gambling, doesn't mean I'm going to do the same to murder."

Ducker jumped out of his chair as two patrolmen entered the area dragging in a noisy drunk. Ducker thumbed towards the door. "Let's get outta here."

The two marched back down the hall, past the Acting Chief's office, past the station desk and the now empty donut box, and out the front door.

They no sooner got into Pope's car and slammed the doors shut when Ducker let loose. "So what the fuck do you want us to do? Go after the entire goddam Cleveland Syndicate just because they packed away some little shit-ball who was probably double-crossing them? You know as well as I do, that's the reason they dumped him in a nightgown. You have no idea what you're up against. It's a lot more complicated than you think—the mayor, the city council—they're all playing this game and you'll be fighting this battle all by yourself."

"Yeah, yeah, I know," Pope replied. He started the engine and pulled out onto Fourth Street. "I'm not as dumb as you think."

Ducker kept his mouth shut and stared ahead.

Pope continued, "But what about Carl Jules? The guy's a classy businessman, even if he's got gambling in his club—so does every other dry cleaner and candy store owner in Newport. They deserve to have the police investigate crimes against them, don't they? We've got to enforce the law *some*times. If Carl showed up packed in cement, I'd say, yeah, it's mob-related. But how do you know this wasn't personal?"

Ducker made a face. "Okay. I suppose it could be the wife." He nodded thoughtfully. "Found out her 'classy' husband had a piece of ass while he was working late. Wouldn't be the first time."

Pope went south on Route 9. Ten minutes later, they were pulling up to the radio patrol car barricading the driveway that led up to The Oasis. Two patrolmen, jackets unbuttoned and ties loosened, slouched against the side of the car. One yawned and stretched, the other tossed a penknife at the ground, sticking it in the dirt. They both straightened up and approached Pope's car as he brought it to a halt.

Ducker said, "We've got the case. Gonna do some poking around here for a while. Anyone been by?"

"Naw," the yawner replied.

Pope and Ducker drove around the patrol car and headed for the back door where Carl Jules had been found.

As usual, Pope was startled by the sight of The Oasis. It was a square, stucco building with a white domed roof that reflected the morning sunlight. It was completely out of place —something you might see in Casablanca, not in the bluegrass hills of Kentucky, where you were more likely to stumble upon moonshine stills left over from Prohibition days.

The back door was still open, and a small stain marked the spot where Carl Jules had fallen.

Pope said, "The guy must've been hit soon as he opened the door. Whoever shot him didn't give him a chance to take one more step."

The detectives made note of the bullet holes they found around the door frame, before searching the parking lot. Starting from the door, Pope and Ducker made a methodical, semi-circular sweep of the lot, walking from opposite directions so they crossed paths and double-checked each other.

Thirty minutes into their search, Ducker called out, "I've had enough of this shit, let's go back to the station. This is a waste of time."

"No, it isn't." Pope said, and kept on looking. Fifteen minutes later, he found seven brass bullet casings about ninety feet away from the door. Pope took out a pen, marked down the evidence on a white envelope, signed his name, and scooped the brass into the envelope.

———

11:00 A.M.

"OH MY GOD!" Ginnie Stevenson stared at the morning edition of the *Kentucky Times-Star.* She was still in her pajamas, having breakfast in the kitchen of the rooming house she shared with five other chorus girls. Her head was pounding from the flask of bourbon she'd drunk the night before.

Vera Kowalski, one of her housemates, looked over Ginnie's shoulder and read the headline: CLUB OWNER SHOT "Who was shot?"

Hand to her mouth, Ginnie ignored her and read the entire article.

"What's happened?"

Ginnie stared into her cup of coffee.

"Oh, give me that," Vera said, grabbing the newspaper out of Ginnie's hands. She quickly scanned the first paragraph. "Cripes! That's your boss. Bet it was Red Masterson and his boys who did it. Was there any trouble at the club last night?"

Ginnie looked up, tears in her eyes. "I was talking to him—must've been just a half hour before it happened."

"So now what? Think they'll shut down the club?"

"I don't know."

"Well, I know we've got enough dancers at the Primrose, but you could try over at the Beverly Hills."

"You really think I'll be out of a job? They *have* to keep the club going. Joey can run things until his father gets better. He's here for another week."

Vera tapped the newspaper with her chipped red fingernail. "Says here, Mr. Jules is still unconscious. Doesn't sound good to me. I think you better get a jump on the other gals and start looking for a new job."

"No. Joey loves The Oasis, he won't let it close. He'll stay and run it."

"There's a war going on, honey. Or did you forget?"

"The Navy'll let him go. I heard of a family whose boy won't get drafted because he's their only son. They won't take the only male capable of carrying on a family's bloodline."

Vera laughed. "Where did you hear *that?* The way you and your precious Joey have been going at it these last three days, I wouldn't worry about the Jules bloodline." She wagged her finger at Ginnie. "Be careful. You might give them a new little prince before the war's over."

9

POPE AND DUCKER STUDIED the two bullets dug out of Carl Jules that morning, comparing them with the five they'd found at the scene.

"Seems like they're the same caliber to me," Pope said.

Ducker screwed up one side of his face. "Yeah. Could be."

Pope took out the envelope containing the brass he'd collected at The Oasis parking lot, and carefully shook its contents onto his desk. "Seven slugs. Seven casings. They look like .380s." He used the sharpened end of his pencil to pick up a casing. "But this one isn't... it's marked 9MM CORTO. That's Italian made." Pope checked the other six. "So are these."

Ducker shrugged. "Yeah, so?"

Pope chewed on his lower lip, trying to hold his temper in check. I'm not going to let his heel-dragging keep me from doing my job, he thought.

Pope gathered up the fruits of their morning's labor, put them back into their respective envelopes, and went down the hall to knock on Acting Chief Gugel's door.

Gugel was shuffling the ever-present pile of paper on his desk. Without looking up, he said, "Yes, Pope?"

"We've got something to send to the FBI for prints."

The Chief didn't answer. In fact, he didn't even look up.

Pope related the morning's activity to him anyway. The Chief kept his eyes down and continued reading something on his desk, underlining here and there with his gold fountain pen.

Pope stopped talking and waited, wondering if Gugel knew he was still there. Finally, Gugel looked up, took in a deep breath, and exhaled slowly.

The apathetic look on the Chief's face told Pope he was in for more heel-dragging, so he spoke up again before the session could start. "Sir. Carl Jules has a lot of friends on city council. I expect you'd want to reassure them that this police department is doing all it can to track down whoever is responsible for gunning down this well-respected businessman." He paused.

Gugel just stared at him through half-closed eyes.

"And you know it's going to take maybe a month to get results back."

Gugel kept staring at Pope. Finally, he smirked. "Send it off."

Pope smiled to himself as he left the office. He felt good about successfully maneuvering around the bought-and-paid-for inertia. But only for a brief moment. As he stuffed his hands in his pockets and swaggered back down the hall to the squadroom, he felt his money clip, now thick with five tens. His stomach tensed. For some things, he, too, had a price.

Burying "the gift" in a safe deposit box wasn't going to make him feel any cleaner.

CLAUDETTE WINKED at Old Man Garvey, plunked down some silver for cigarettes and a newspaper, and walked out of Garvey's Groceries reading the front page. Below the story headlined: **CLUB OWNER SHOT**, was a second story that caught her eye: **COPS FISH SMALL FRY HOOD FROM RIVER**

Boy, she thought, Bruno's been very busy this past week. Actually, Claudette was surprised. Bruno had come to see her last night and had seemed excited about something—more aroused than usual—but she hadn't picked up the feeling that he was priming himself for a hit. Their sessions were usually foreplay to a violent and, for him, more satisfying climax. She wondered if she was losing her ability to read clients. The thought made her feel insecure. Claudette decided to head back up Monmouth Street to her room and do a Tarot card reading for herself.

But first she'd deposit the twenty bucks Bruno slipped her last night into her bank account.

BRUNO CARPELLA STROLLED DOWN York Street, mentally going over his list, checking off those who had just crossed over into the past due column. Some, he'd just have to twist their arms to jog their memories and get them to pay up. Others would be harder to find—those guys were asking to have a thumb busted here, a pinkie broken there.

His thoughts turned to Carl Jules. Now was the time to put a little pressure on the rest of the family, make them realize it made good business sense to sell The Oasis.

———

LOGBOOK ENTRY: 1100 Hours

I LAY IN BED, trying to orient myself. It took me a couple of minutes to remember where I was. First off, some half-assed bugle boy didn't wake me up by trying to blow revelry like Harry James running through *Flight of the Bumblebee*. Second, my bed wasn't a hammock or a hard bunk. Third, the walls weren't made of metal and I wasn't surrounded by a dozen snoring seamen. It was really quiet.

I lay there in a big brass bed in the guest room Joey had stashed me in, and listened for sounds in the house. Nobody was up. Hoisting my legs over the bedside, I almost stepped on my seabag. I rummaged inside, pulled out my work trousers and a white cotton shirt—the only set of civvies I owned—and got dressed.

I didn't know what to do next. Roaming around someone else's house while they slept in their beds would feel strange, like I was some kind of cat burglar. Seeing a desk in one corner of the room, I decided to do some writing. I'd been too bushed the night before to make an entry in my logbook, so I killed the next half hour catching up—it took a lot of words to record the dramatic events of the previous day.

When I finished, I screwed the top back on my pen, blotted the last few lines, and closed my logbook. Downstairs, a door opened, then closed. I remembered Joey telling me their housekeeper would be coming in just before noon. Hopefully, that meant I could get some chow soon—I was starving.

There were bookshelves mounted on the wall above the desk where I sat. I scanned the rows of book spines, reading the titles. Nothing interested me until I got to a stack of old pulps. Corny as it sounds, my heart leapt for joy and did a series of handsprings. It was like finding a piece of myself— a happy piece of my childhood. I stood up and picked the top magazine off the pile. It was a copy of *Adventure*, an issue I remembered poring over when I was about twelve years old. On the cover, in garish colors, a bloodied French Legionnaire was locked in hand-to-hand combat with some sword-swinging Arab as they both slid and tumbled down a sand dune. It might have even been that very issue that made me want to become a writer.

Reading those magazines had taken me out of the dark little bedroom I shared with my younger brother. I'd dream of the day when I could go off and have my own adventures and write about them. The adventures I'd had so far, though, didn't match up to the ones I imagined as a kid.

Footsteps in the hallway announced there was life in the house. I put the magazine back on the stack, and headed for the door. There was a knock, followed by, "Hey, Nick. You awake?"

I opened the door to Joey and the smells of freshly brewed coffee and frying bacon.

Joey looked me up and down, tilted his head back and frowned. "We can do better than this, Nick."

"What?" I asked, wondering why he was offended.

"Those clothes. We'll go down to Monmouth Street and fix you up with some duds."

WE WERE SITTING at the breakfast table drinking orange juice when Pearl came down. Her eyes were puffy and she didn't have any lipstick on. But she still looked gorgeous.

She sat down across the table from me, next to Joey, who leaned over and kissed her cheek. I wished I were in his place. Goddammit, where was my head? I swallowed hard and said, "Morning, Mrs. Jules."

"Good morning, Nick. Hope you boys slept better than I did. I'm real anxious to get back to the hospital."

"Ma, first have some breakfast," Joey said. "Then we'll get right over there."

Pearl nibbled halfheartedly at a piece of toast, and spent the next ten minutes pushing the scrambled eggs and bacon around on the plate that Flora, their Negro housekeeper, had set before her.

I was halfway through my eggs, when Pearl's fork clattered on her plate. "Okay, boys," she said, "I'm ready to go."

I started shoveling the remainder of my breakfast into my mouth. The front doorbell rang.

Pearl jumped up. "I'll get it."

She was gone for a minute, then came back into the

kitchen. "Joey, there are two detectives in the parlor. They want a statement from you about what happened to your father last night."

"Me?" Joey said. "I wasn't there."

"So that's what you tell them."

He groaned and pushed away from the table. "Okay."

Pearl paced up and down the kitchen, waiting for Joey to come back. I just sat there, watching her, but I didn't want to be too obvious about it, so I looked away. My eyes rested on a plaque hanging on the wall. It had flowers and sheep painted around its edges, and the center was filled with gold lettering. Silently, I started to read: *The Lord is my Shepherd, I shall not want—*

Oh, jeez.

It was a very long fifteen minutes before Joey poked his head back in.

"Hey, Nick. The cops want to talk to you."

Pearl wheeled around, looked at me and then back at Joey. "What for?" She and I said in unison.

Joey shrugged. "Beats me."

THE DETECTIVES INTRODUCED themselves to me as Pope and Ducker.

The one named Pope said, "Just some quick questions, Mr. Cavanaugh." And then proceeded to ask me what train I came in on, when I got in, who picked me up. The interrogation didn't even take five minutes and then they were gone.

SHORTLY AFTER THAT, we were driving to the hospital in the Cadillac, Pearl sitting between me and Joey in the front seat. I kept my eyes trained out the windshield, but was quietly going nuts breathing in the scent of this lady beside me.

Joey broke the silence. "Ma, I'll stay with you a while at the hospital, but then I'm going to take Nick to Monmouth Street and get him suited up."

Pearl nodded. "Fine, but I want you at the club tonight. Get over there in time for the dinner show. Make sure that singer from New York doesn't get too drunk to go on."

I leaned forward and looked past Pearl, "Joey, I don't need anything."

Both mama and son turned to me. Pearl said, "Yes, you do. No offense meant." She gave me a little smile. "Sorry all this has happened. Don't let it keep you from having a good time."

I turned away from her—figured if she could read in my eyes what I was thinking, she'd kick me out of the car right then and there.

WE FOUND HUNCH WILLIAMS standing guard outside Mr. Jules' private hospital room almost in the same spot we'd left him that morning, five hours earlier.

Pearl told him, "Go home and get some sleep."

"I will, after my backup arrives." Hunch jerked his head towards the room. "Nothing's changed."

Pearl nodded. "Okay." She breathed in and then let it out, the weight on her shoulders almost visible. "Hunch, you're in charge at the club tonight." A thought suddenly hit. Her eyes flashed. "*Oh, damn.* Better check with the cops to make sure they're not keeping the place closed for some reason, like pretending to look for evidence."

"Yeah. Don't worry about it, Doc and I'll keep things running."

"You'll have Joey, too."

Hunch gave Joey a nod as mother and son entered the room. I hung back in the corridor and watched them approach the bed. Mr. Jules didn't appear to know anybody was there. Pearl bent over his body and kissed him on his forehead. Then, she then got down on her knees beside the bed and crossed herself. Joey turned away and stared out the window, I guessed to give her privacy.

I sensed Hunch watching me, and I figured it was best to keep my back to him. He was definitely the family's guard dog and, if he was a halfway decent one, he'd sniff out the fact that I wanted to hold his mistress in my arms and comfort her. It was time for me to take a walk.

I found a chair and a tattered copy of *The Saturday Evening Post* at the end of the hallway and sat there, scanning through the articles and short stories. That seemed to calm Hunch down, though I suppose it was just paranoia that had me thinking he was snarling at me in the first place. The guy that came and took over for him fifteen minutes later wasn't nearly as effective-looking. Shortly after that, Joey came out of the room, said a few words to the new guy, looked around, saw me and walked towards me. I jumped up.

"Okay, Nick. Let's shove off." Joey's face was grim.

"How's it lookin'?"

"My Dad?" Joey shook his head. "I'm going to find the bastard who did this to him and kill him." He kept his eyes on the ground as we made our way out of the hospital and into the parking lot. As we reached the Cadillac, I remembered Joey lying to Pearl about his father letting him take the car. I also remembered Joey saying he was late picking me up at the train station because he'd had a fight with his dad. Now here he was, vowing revenge. Guess for some sons and fathers, blood *was* thicker than water. A twinge of envy shot through me, but I shook it off.

In the car, I turned to Joey and said, "Why'd you lie to your mother last night?"

Joey swung a look at me. "Huh? What're you talking about?"

"About your dad letting you have the Caddy to come pick me up."

"Oh, that. Hell, I feel shitty enough as it is." Joey turned the key in the ignition. "With all that's happened, I didn't want her to know me and Pop had words. I can be a real schmuck sometimes."

Joey shifted into gear, pulled out of the parking lot, and headed for Newport. At one point on our short drive, we came alongside the Ohio River and I looked out across to the other side at the skyline of Cincinnati. I imagined her skyscrapers looking down their noses at me and thought about my own dad. Just ahead of us was the Central Bridge linking Newport to Cincinnati. A right turn would take me back. Joey took a left, the Cadillac throwing dust up into the Queen City's face. That was fine with me—I wasn't ready to cross that bridge.

We drove south on Washington, then headed back up Monmouth. Traffic was heavy and parking spots were scarce. Joey saw a couple of young gals getting into a car, and stopped in the middle of the street to wait for them to leave. He was deaf. The drivers, lined up behind us, started honking their horns and shouting obscenities at us but, eventually, we got a spot right in front of Saul's Tailoring.

Saul was a little round man in a white shirt, sleeves rolled up to his elbows. He also wore a black vest, unbuttoned, and a matching cloth skullcap that must have been glued to the top of his bald head. A yellow tape measure hung around his neck like a thin prayer shawl.

"Joey, Joey, Joey!" The man came towards us, arms outstretched in a greeting.

"Hi, Saul." Joey extended his hand.

The little guy shook Joey's hand and pulled him into a hug. "What a wonderful surprise." Saul stepped back. "I'm so very sorry about your father. Terrible, terrible. How's your mother?"

"Ma's a tough lady."

"Don't I know it. What do the doctors say?"

Joey filled him in, repeating the same information that Pearl told Hunch and Doc the previous night—basically that, "nobody knows nothin'." Then he introduced me and my problem. "Got anything to spiff up this big lug pal of mine?"

Saul squinted up at me. "Hmm. I'd say you're a forty-five long." He slipped the tape measure from around his neck and snapped it around my waist. "Thirty-five." He kicked a scuffed wooden box from under a table and stepped on it to measure my neck and sleeves. "You're a big guy, but I got some suits that'll fit you."

Saul started pulling jackets and trousers off the rack and laying them across a table.

Joey said, "Hey, Saul. You hear all the scuttlebutt on the street. Anything about my Pop?"

"Like what?" Saul handed me a jacket. "Try this on just for fit."

Joey shrugged. "I don't know. I've been away for over a year. Things happen. People get angry with each other. Anyone got a grudge against him?"

"You know as well as I do, not everyone's crying about what happened to your father. In fact, just 'bout a half hour ago, I saw Sleepout Louie walking down the street with those two brothers of his reading the newspaper and laughing his head off. And I don't think it was *Blondie* that was tickling his funny bone." Saul dropped a pair of pants on the table to accent his point.

I had to get in on the conversation. "Who's Sleepout Louie?"

Saul answered, "He and his brothers run the Flamingo over on York Street and—"

"They're a bunch of goddamn fat assholes," Joey said, in a loud voice. "Probably taking bets right now on when The Oasis closes up shop." He looked out the door and shouted, "I got news for 'em all. It ain't gonna happen."

Saul walked quickly over to my pal. "Hey, Joey. Shhh, don't go crazy. That's not going to help your father or your mother."

Joey hitched up the lapels of his sports jacket and I got a glimpse of the butt of the automatic nestled under his armpit. So did Saul, who put a friendly hand on Joey's shoulder. "Don't go crazy."

"Yeah, yeah." Joey nodded and took out a cigarette. "Hey, Nick. You look like a big shot in that jacket."

The next hour was spent marking up sleeves for lengthening and pant legs for cuffs, picking out shirts and ties, and trying on shoes and snap brims. Finally, Saul said, "Come back around seven and the suit'll be ready. The sports jacket and trousers, tomorrow."

We left Saul's and strolled down Monmouth Street. It was a warm, breezy day, good for looking at the pretty girls out window shopping. Every once in a while, a breeze would pick up the hem of a skirt in front of us, and we'd get a peek at a pair of legs that were just as shapely as Betty Grable's back at the barracks. Joey and I got our fair share of silent whistles, too—one of the few times I've seen any good in being stuck state-side. There ain't much competition.

On our way down the street, Joey pointed out storefronts and cafés on both sides, accompanied by a running commentary. "There's lay-off betting going on in there," he said. "That one's a bustout joint. I wouldn't trust the dice in those two across the street."

Nothing was as it seemed—at least half the businesses had minor-league gambling in their back rooms.

Joey nodded up the street. "See that place, the Glenn Hotel?"

I saw a sign that said GLENN HOTEL in letters running vertically down the side of a three-story building. Over the front entrance, spelled out on a marquee, was GLENN RENDEZVOUS.

Joey said, "See the man standing out in front? That's Pete Schmidt. He's an independent, like my Pop." He hesitated for a moment. "But I wouldn't call him a friend of the family."

As we got closer, the man turned, saw Joey, and bobbed his head in a greeting. Pete Schmidt didn't seem like the friendly type, his facial muscles looked as if they'd been frozen in a glower for years.

I think Joey intended to just walk on by, because he seemed surprised when Schmidt followed up his head bob with, "Tell your Ma, it's just the beginning."

Joey stopped dead in his tracks. "What d'ya mean by that?"

"Come here," Schmidt said, and waited for us to walk the few steps over to him as if he didn't want to speak too loudly. He turned his hard look up at me, and asked Joey, "Who's your buddy here?"

Joey answered, "Petty officer third class Nick Cavanaugh. He's my partner on Shore Patrol."

"Oh. Another sailor boy." No handshakes were offered. Schmidt turned his attention to Joey. "You know as well as I do what's going on here. Same battles we been fighting the past eight years—only your Pa thought those Cleveland Jew Boys would leave him alone just because his place is out there in the hills. Well, that sure as hell didn't stop them from burning my first place down to the ground."

Schmidt eyed me. "You from around here?"

I said, "Not anymore. Grew up across the river. Left there years ago."

"Hmm. Let me tell you what they did to me. I started with nothing but a fuckin' one-horse cart. I'd haul anything. Worked my way up to driving bootleg trucks for old George Remus. You know who he is? Never mind." He turned to Joey. "That's how I met your Pa, he was driving for Remus, too. I wound up going to jail 'cause of Remus, but not Carl Jules— he slipped through somehow." Schmidt looked back at me. "Got the name 'Lucky Jules' for that. Anyway, I had enough stashed away to buy this place as soon as I got out," he said, jerking his thumb over his shoulder at the hotel, "—even had a thousand-gallon-a-day still in operation outside of town. Went to jail for that, too. But you think this was all I wanted? Naw, I had big plans—still do. Game's not over yet."

Schmidt took a breath, and pointed south. "You been over to the Beverly Hills? That was mine. Those Jews stole it from me. I bought that hill and the old Kaintuck Castle nightclub on top of it, gutted the place and turned the joint into a real swanky casino. Then I—" He suddenly stopped, eyes focused on something moving behind me on the street.

Both Joey and I turned to see what had caught his attention. Must have been the maroon convertible—or rather, the big guy driving it.

Joey knew immediately who he was, and added to the wealth of information I'd been accumulating over the past twelve hours. "That's Red Masterson. He's the Syndicate's 'Enforcer'."

Schmidt said, "That's the bastard who burned my Beverly Hills—the first one—right down to the ground. But I rebuilt it bigger and better. Then he puts the pressure on, harassed me for the next four years—used six hoods armed with submachine guns to steal my club's bankroll. I had to bring in hired gunmen from out of town. Cleveland spread the word around to the other mobs to cut me off. Shit, I wound up having to hire Negroes. I even paid a mob from Toledo to run the Beverly for me, but they quit. I couldn't make a go of it—had to sell out."

The muscles around Pete Schmidt's mouth hardened, and his glower was even more pronounced—if that was possible. "That sonofabitch Red Masterson was part of the gang with me, an' Carl, an' Buck Brady—at least a dozen of us made up the old Remus Ring." He cleared his throat and spat out a gray oyster. "George Remus. Back in the twenties, we controlled almost *fifteen percent* of all the bonded whiskey in the United States. Now we're all hustling for small change. Remus is with Buck over at the Primrose. Red is licking the hand of those *kikes* upstate. Me—I ain't finished yet. I'll get back on top. Got plans. Big ones."

Schmidt spun on his heels and started back into his hotel, ignoring us as though we were nothing more than cracks on the sidewalk. Just as he reached for the door, he stopped and called over his shoulder, "Yeah, we used to call Carl, 'Lucky Jules'—but I think his luck's just about run out."

10

CLAUDETTE SAT ON HER BED, pulled her dress up over her knees, and crossed her legs. She heard the Oxydol jingle coming from the radio in the next room. Millie, another of Sophie's girls, was listening to *Ma Perkins*, her favorite soap opera.

Claudette shuffled the deck of Tarot cards, anxiety bubbling in her stomach. She was confused. How could she have misread Bruno last night? That had never happened before. She hated to even *think* her ability was weakening. But she felt different—restless, like something was about to change.

Claudette looked around her room, unable to imagine how that change was going to take place. A tiny voice whispered inside her head, *You're going to be stuck here forever.* She shook that off, knowing if she listened to that voice she might as well crawl under her bed and wait for the rats to eat her.

She closed her eyes and pictured herself at Union Terminal, boarding a train heading west to a new beginning. Claudette still believed that day was coming. The cards would reveal what was in store.

She tried to shut out the sound of the radio, clear her mind of all distracting thoughts and focus on the questions: When am I going to get out of here? How will that happen? As she continued shuffling, she repeated the questions in her mind, preparing herself for the reading.

Mid-shuffle, a card popped out and landed face-up in front of her. Claudette looked down at the card with great interest, knowing it would be significant.

She whistled. It was The Fool card. Potential. Opportunity. New beginnings. Time for a change. But she also remembered the warning: *Beware of The Fool's appearance in a reading. He is a challenge to tread warily.*

Claudette reached under the bed and grabbed her book. She flipped through the well-worn pages to the description of The Fool, skimmed through what she'd already memorized, then stopped to read: *An unexpected opportunity may appear out of the blue. A new relationship may be about to start, or an unconventional person may enter your life. The people you meet now may be participants in a new phase of your life.*

Heavy footsteps on the stairs interrupted her. Claudette

tensed. It was too early for customers. She turned her ear towards the door. The footsteps moved too fast to be Sophie's—besides, she was out doing her shopping.

No, they were the footsteps of men. Two of them.

Claudette listened to them clomp past her door and down to the end of the hallway. Doors opened and banged shut. She jumped out of bed to see what was going on.

Just as she poked her head out into the hallway, she saw two large men—one in a rumpled brown suit, the other in a loud checkered sports jacket—open Millie's door, next to hers, and look in. Millie screamed.

Claudette shouted, "Who the hell are you? Get out of here!"

The bigger of the two, the one in the rumpled brown suit, gave her a broken-toothed grin and said, in a hoarse voice, "That must be her."

Claudette felt a sudden twinge of fear deep inside, and quickly stepped back into her room, pulling on the door. Before she could slam it shut, the brown suit stuck his foot in the door and pushed it open with his shoulder, knocking her off balance. Claudette stumbled backwards, but caught herself. *Gotta stay on my feet.*

The second guy entered the room, slammed the door behind him and stood with his back against it, barring her escape.

"Mill—" Claudette screamed. The brown suit's hand clamped over her face, shutting off her cry for help. And her air supply. First, she'd smelled the tobacco on his hand, then she was suffocating. Still on her feet, Claudette struggled, pounding on the thug's arm, trying to weaken his grasp.

The guy at the door called out, "Manny! We're here to

fuck her, not kill her."

Manny slid his hand down, uncovering Claudette's nostrils. She sucked in air, and tried to kick Manny's balls out his ass, but she didn't have the leverage. He laughed and, without much effort, pushed her down on the bed with his hand still clamped over her mouth. As he straddled her, Claudette froze with a terror that overwhelmed the anger she'd felt just seconds before.

Manny snorted. "You scared? How come? You're just a prostitute. You do this every night with all kinds of little-dick johns. Betcha ain't never had it like I'm gonna give it to ya."

But those little dicks come on *my* terms, Claudette thought as she felt a second surge of anger. A *fuck you* flashed out her eyes.

"Hey, Al," he said, "Bruno's right. She's got real pretty green eyes."

Bruno? thought Claudette. *He* sent them? How could he do this to her?

Manny said, "You gonna be quiet? I don't want to hurt you. I'll let go of your mouth if you promise not to holler."

Claudette nodded. When her mouth was free, she said, "Bruno sent you?"

"Yeah," Al called over from his post at the door. "Well, not exactly. He's our boss. Been telling us about you for so long, we just had to come by to sample the wares ourselves. We'll even pay for it." He pulled out a couple of tens and threw them on the bed. "Bet we're better in the sack than he is."

Well that sure wouldn't take much, Claudette said to herself. They were nothing but a couple of stupid little boys. She pushed against Manny's chest. "Get the fuck off, you're breaking my legs."

Caught off guard, Manny did so.

Claudette sat up in bed. "I don't care how good you are, we're not open. This isn't a day house. Come back during regular business hours. We open tonight at seven."

"We can't," Al said, "we're working."

Claudette threw back her head and laughed until tears trickled from the corners of her eyes. Bruno's dumb-ass loser pals.

Manny grabbed her ankles, pulling her legs apart like a wishbone. Claudette's laugh turned into a high-pitched scream. Manny lunged to a kneeling position, his knees grinding into her thighs, pinning them down. "You bitch, I'm horny *now!*" he shouted, clenching her wrists above her head with one hand, and undoing his pants with the other.

Dread filled Claudette again as she realized she'd misread these two just as she had Bruno.

Al hurried over. "I want to see those tits Bruno's been yapping about." He ripped open the top of her dress, sending the tiny buttons bouncing and skittering across the hardwood floor. Claudette screamed again as he yanked on her silk camisole, tearing it from its straps. "*Whoo-ee!* Look at those!"

Claudette cringed and her stomach turned as she felt Al's sweaty hand on her skin.

Manny shoved Al away. "She's mine. Go stand at the door."

Claudette aimed a scream out her open window, "Millie! Sophie! Help—"

Manny slapped her across the face so hard it made her head buzz. "I told you to shut the fuck up."

"You're going to have to kill me," she replied, half dazed, and tried to thrust her legs up to kick the bastard away from her. But she didn't have the strength. He was so big and close to her face, his wide shoulders and chest filled her field of vision, blocking most of the room from view. She could just see a corner of her room and the top of the bedroom door.

The door swung open and Claudette heard it slam against something hard.

Al, holding his head, staggered backwards into her field of vision.

Manny turned. "What the—"

A fist, holding an automatic pistol, swung up over Manny's shoulder and down onto his head. Claudette heard the crunch of metal smashing against bone. She scooted out from underneath Manny and got to her feet, as he crumpled onto the bed. Joey Jules jumped on top of Manny and pistol-whipped him.

Suddenly, the room was full of people. Sophie stood at the door holding a baseball bat, a wide-eyed Millie peeked over her shoulder, and a very tall man Claudette had never seen before had Al immobilized with his arms pinned behind his back.

The very tall man shouted, "Think he got the point, Joey."

Joey stopped pounding, looked at Manny's bloodied face, then gave him one last vicious whack. "And that one's for my Pop."

———

LOGBOOK ENTRY:

At THAT MOMENT, I wondered if I better let go of the guy I had in an arm lock and grab Joey to keep him from killing the fella on the bed. But Joey stopped on his own.

The girl seemed okay. She stood in the middle of the room, clutching her dress to keep it closed over her breasts.

Sophie marched over to where I stood and pointed the barrel of her baseball bat right into the face of the guy I was holding.

"Don't you ever come back here. If I see you or your pal anywhere on this block—all I have to say is a couple of words to Red."

"We were going to pay, see?" I followed the guy's nod towards the bed. There were two crumpled bills lying on top of the sheets. Also, some kind of picture cards were scattered all over the bed and on the floor around it.

Sophie shook her bat under his nose. "You know how things work around here. This ain't about money—you don't come storming into *my* house and treat *my* girls like dirt. They got houses down by the river for the likes of you. This ain't the 'Bottoms'—take your business down there."

I could feel the guy shaking—but I don't think he was doing so just on account of Sophie. Joey had joined us and it was obvious he was just barely controlling his anger. He was fidgety, but his eyes had a cold, focused look as he rolled the grip of his automatic in his hand.

I asked Sophie, "What do you want us to do with these guys?"

"Throw the trash out."

"Okay. Joey, you take this guy." I handed him over and went to the bed. Bending down, I grabbed the bloodied bastard by his armpits, and lifted until I could hoist him over my shoulder. Joey and the shaky one led the way. I followed, carrying the sack of shit from the bedroom, down the stairs, and out of the house, depositing him on the curb. There he finally started coming to. His playmate took over, and helped him walk down the block towards York Street, ignoring the stares of passing pedestrians.

Joey and I kept guard from the front steps of Sophie's house until they were out of sight.

As we went back inside, I said to Joey, "So those two guys are connected with the Cleveland mob? Don't you think beating on them will make them want to hit back at your family even harder?"

"Shit, don't matter to me." Then seeing the shocked look on my face, he waved his hand in the air. "Nah, don't worry. I know those guys. Manny'll lick his wounds, Al will get a little nervous. But it's got nothing to do with The Oasis. Red Masterson'll just chew both their asses for messing with one of Sophie's girls to begin with. That is, if they admit to it in the first place."

We found Sophie, Claudette, and Millie in the parlor. On my first trip into the house, I'd been running as fast as I could to get up the stairs and hadn't taken any notice of the surroundings. This was obviously a high class place—for a bordello. Red velvet drapes hung at the front windows and were tied open with gold ropes, the knobs of their tassels as big as my fist.

Claudette sprawled on a green velvet sofa—a fancy piece of furniture with carved wood trim curling across the back. The walls were covered with paintings in ornate gold frames. They looked like old masters. On a quick study, I realized there was a basic theme to the artwork—more sprawling women, all sultry smiles and round, naked flesh.

Sophie poured a brandy. She handed it to Claudette.

Millie said, "I need one, too."

"No, you don't," Sophie shot back. "Go make some tea."

As Claudette sipped her brandy, Sophie fussed over her, plumping up pillows and stuffing them behind her back. "There, is that better? Are you comfortable?" Sophie asked her.

Not that Claudette didn't deserve to be fussed over. Prostitute or not, no woman deserved to be whacked around. But she didn't seem much the worse for wear. She was small-boned, barely over five feet tall, and had porcelain skin that looked like it would crack if a man handled it too roughly. But her green eyes flashed with some kind of inner strength—the same toughness I'd sensed in Joey's mother.

What was it that made these Kentucky women so fiery? That Manny was damn lucky he didn't make the mistake of forcing her to give him oral sex 'cause, sure as hell, she'd have bit off his dick. For a moment, I considered the possibility that maybe Joey and I had arrived a minute too early, and her attacker had escaped the punishment he *really* deserved.

Claudette aimed those green peepers at me over her shot of brandy. I don't exactly know what she was thinking, and I wasn't about to ask, but she lingered on me. Then, turning to Joey, she said, "I'm really grateful you boys showed up. How did Millie find y'all?"

Joey tipped his hat back up his forehead. "Nick and I were just on our way over here from the Glenn Rendezvous across the street. We'd been shooting the breeze with Pete Schmidt and decided to come talk to Sophie."

"And I was just heading home when I bumped into them on the corner," Sophie said, refilling Claudette's glass.

Millie, who never did leave the room to make tea, said, "That's where I found them. When those men closed the door on you, I didn't know what to do. So I ran out of the house and down the street, thinking I'll find a cop over at the Glenn Rendezvous, and then I saw Sophie talking to these two gentlemen."

Claudette's eyebrow arched slightly at the word "gentlemen." She exchanged a half-smile with Joey, then raised her glass of brandy. "And so the cavalry comes to the rescue in the nick of time."

"The Navy," I said.

"Joey, you haven't introduced me to your friend, yet."

Joey smiled and wriggled his eyebrows at me. "Claudette, allow me to introduce you to Mister In-the-Nick-of-Time, himself. This is my shipmate, Nick Cavanaugh."

Joey's cornball joke touched off a raucous laugh from Sophie and squeezed out a line of giggles from Millie.

Claudette saluted me with her drink, an amused look on her face. She was quite something. If I'd walked in just then, I would never have guessed she'd just gone through some harrowing experience.

Joey and I stuck around for another hour "just in case," as he put it. With Joey, that could mean he was half-expecting those two thugs to come back with some friends, or that he was waiting for Claudette to invite him upstairs to show her gratitude. Neither happened. But we *were* joined by the four other "ladies of the house" who were in a boisterous mood after spending the afternoon at the Coney Island amusement park. And we did find out from Sophie, who was plugged into every grapevine in Newport, that Carl Jules hadn't made any new enemies. Nor had any new feuds flared up in the year and a half since Joey joined the navy and was shipped across country.

Guess these days a lot of bad news traveled along those grapevines, too. Sophie told Joey about an old schoolmate of his who'd been killed in North Africa, fighting Rommel and his panzer divisions. Then she asked if we'd heard any more about the action on the Pacific front than what the newspapers reported. "My nephew's a marine," she said, "and his mother's sick with worry 'cause she hasn't gotten a letter from him in a month. Name's Tim Clark. Maybe you know him?"

We didn't. And we didn't have any more information about the fighting in the islands than she did. Of course, even if we did know something, we would have kept our mouths shut—loose lips sink ships.

Our impromptu tea party came to an end. As Joey was saying his goodbyes to Sophie and her gals, Claudette called me over with a little tilt of her head. She reached out her hand. When I took it, she gave mine a squeeze and said, in a soft voice, "Feel free to drop anchor here any time before seven. No charge."

11

GINNIE STEVENSON WALKED DOWN the street to the
corner drugstore to buy some shampoo. It had been a horrible
afternoon. All her housemates wanted to talk about was the
shooting. And about where she might go for work. Ginnie
stated, until she was blue in the face, that she wasn't going to
leave The Oasis until they shut down. She didn't want to think
Vera might be right when she said, "That could happen next
week."

The few days she'd had with Joey had been perfect.
She just wanted her life to go on forever like that—working at

The Oasis and being with Joey. Ginnie couldn't leave, go look for another job. She had to believe that everything would get back to the way it was. Joey would be able to keep things going until Carl was better.

A little bell jingled as she pushed open the door and entered the drugstore.

It was easy for Vera to say, "Go look for another job." But Ginnie wasn't like all the other dancers in town, changing jobs as easily as they changed costumes. Dancing at The Oasis had been her first real job and she intended to stay there. She didn't like change.

But things *had* changed. Ginnie tried to push the thought away, but couldn't—she kept seeing Joey's cocky smile as he opened the door of the dealers' break room with one hand and zipped up his fly with the other.

As she paid for her bottle of shampoo, Ginnie told herself, *Just put one foot in front of the other and things will eventually right themselves.* She'd go home, wash her hair, get dressed for work, and carry on as if nothing was different.

The bell jingled again as she opened the door and stepped out onto the sidewalk. The store's entrance was right on the corner of the building, so when you were standing in front of it you didn't know if you were on Monmouth or the side street. There was a clear view of both.

Ginnie froze. Joey Jules and some big lug were coming out of Sophie's whorehouse a few buildings down and across from her on the side street.

"You bastard," she whispered through clenched teeth. She didn't move, just stared at the two men walking towards the corner. Joey was laughing. Ginnie couldn't stand to watch him any longer. She stepped back into the drugstore's recessed entrance, turned, and kept her eyes focused on the *Don Juan Lipstick* ad until Joey's laugh faded away down Monmouth Street.

———

Bruno SAT AT A WINDOW TABLE in the Mecca Cafe & Grill on Monmouth Street, chowing down on his roast beef dinner special. He sawed off a big slab of meat, stuffed it in his mouth, and shoveled in a huge glob of mashed potatoes on top of it. Gravy dribbled down his chin. He stopped it with a wipe of his knuckle, licked his finger, and forked up another chunk of medium rare. Bruno had spent the afternoon making calls on a half dozen delinquent clients. Intimidating people always worked up his appetite. He gulped down some beer. *Ah. Life is good.*

Ignoring the noisy activity in the restaurant—its clatter of dishes and loud conversations—Bruno stared out the window at the world going by. All kinds of people moved about, trudging along the sidewalk, driving down Monmouth Street. They were either coming home from their fancy office buildings across the river in Cincinnati, or going to their shifts at the smoke-belching steel mills on the west side of Newport. Didn't make any difference where they were going or what they were doing, everybody wore the same dulled expression on their face.

Bruno felt sorry for the poor suckers caught in their dead-end jobs—even those working for the war effort. After all, the war was bound to come to an end sometime. Nope. *His* life was on a roll. Bruno took another swallow of beer and belched loudly. Red Masterson had slapped him on the back today and congratulated him on what a good job he'd been doing.

Ah, life wasn't just good, it was great. And it was going to get even better. Bruno chuckled to himself. He'd told Red what he planned to do at The Oasis that night, and Red said it was exactly what he'd do.

Bruno wiped his plate clean with a piece of bread that he stuffed in his mouth and washed down with a swig of beer. He lingered over the rest of his drink and smoked a cigarette, waiting for opening time at Sophie's. A thought occurred to him just then. He wondered if the cops were going to keep The Oasis closed, just in case Carl Jules died. If Carl did die, that would make it a murder scene. He didn't want to waste his time making a trip into the hills, later that night, for nothing. Bruno got up, went over to the pay phone by the coat rack, and called his contact at the police station.

"Hey, Jerry. It's me. What's the word on The Oasis? You keeping it shut?"

"Nope. The Jules family can open or close or do whatever the hell they want. We got a call earlier from their security guy. He's gonna keep the place open. For now."

"Did you get a nice box of cigars for your birthday last week?"

"Yeah, enjoying one right now. Thanks."

"Sure." Bruno hung up and went back to his seat.

At seven o'clock, Bruno gulped down the last drop of beer, paid his bill at the counter, and wound his way around the tables filled with chattering customers. Outside, he pointed himself towards Sophie's and lumbered down the street, cutting a path through the flow of pedestrians.

When he reached the two-story red brick building,

Bruno climbed the steps to the front door, and rang the bell.

A few seconds later, Sophie half-opened the door and peered out. "Oh, it's you. I don't want you coming here anymore." She slammed the door in Bruno's face.

"Hey! What the fuck??" Bruno pounded on the door with his fist. "Sophie! Open up. It's me."

Sophie opened the parlor window. "I know it's you. Get lost."

"What's the problem? What did I do?"

"It's what your sidekicks did."

Bruno stared at her.

"Don't go acting dumb on me and pretend you don't know."

"I don't," Bruno said, extending his arms and shrugging his shoulders. "What happened?"

"You wait right there," Sophie said, and slammed the window shut. Almost immediately, the front door opened again and Sophie filled the entrance with her bulk, arms crossed over her chest. "Those two stupid jerks that're always following you around almost raped Claudette this afternoon."

"What?"

"Yeah, you heard me. They busted into the house, looking specifically for Claudette. Manhandled her, smacked her around. Lucky a couple of friends of mine came by— otherwise, no telling what your guys would've done to her."

"Manny and Al?"

"I don't know their names. I just know they're your garbage." Sophie unfolded her arms and took a step back into the hallway. "They said they heard all about Claudette from you and 'just had to come by to sample the wares' themselves, so I'm holding you responsible." She slammed the door again.

Bruno stood on the top step staring at the front door. He was stunned.

Turning on his heels, he stepped down to the sidewalk and looked up at the window of Claudette's bedroom. *I still want my fuck,* he screamed inside his head.

Bruno paced up and down in front of the house, trying to figure out what to do about Manny and Al. His blood pounded in his head. Sophie was right—they were *his* garbage, and they belonged on the bottom of the river. But he had to be smarter than that. Bruno headed back to the Yorkshire Club.

Manny and Al should have been there already, waiting for him. But they weren't. Bruno went to his corner stool at the bar, ordered a bourbon and lit a cigarette. Where the hell were they?

It was an automatic reflex for Bruno to watch the customers entering the club and familiarize himself with their faces, but he couldn't keep his mind on the job. He was watching his great night fall apart. If Manny and Al didn't show, they'd screw up his plans for The Oasis, too.

Two cigarettes later, Al walked in the door. *Okay,* Bruno told himself, *stay cool, let them explain themselves. Where the hell is Manny? Stay cool.*

Al walked up to Bruno and said, "Uh—" His eyes rolled around looking at everything in the bar except Bruno's face. "Manny's not feeling too good tonight."

Bruno blew a puff of smoke, bouncing it off Al's nose. "Oh, yeah? What's he got? A bellyache?"

Al directed his answer to Bruno's glass of bourbon. "Uh, no. He kinda got beat up. I had to take him to the hospital, and the doc said for him to stay in bed for a little while, until his head clears."

"That's terrible. Who was it? We'll go pay him back."

Al glanced at Bruno, then back to the bourbon. "A couple of sailors—I didn't recognize who they were."

"Oh—so you were there, too." Bruno squinted at Al. "Escaped without a scratch. Hmm, that's interesting. Wait a minute," he said, stubbing out his cigarette, "let's step into my office."

Bruno led the way, past the bar, into the men's room. Inside, Bruno leaned against the door. "Okay, where were you? What's the story?"

"This afternoon we went by Sophie's place just to say hello. That's where we got mugged by those sailors at gunpoint."

Bruno landed a quick left to Al's jaw, sending him flying back against the row of sinks. "Don't give me none of that crap." He followed it with a kick to the groin. Al cried out, doubled over and fell to the floor beneath one of the sinks where he lay in a heap, holding his balls and groaning.

Bruno studied his stooge. Those two dumb asses were going to screw him up real bad—maybe even stop him from working his way up in the Syndicate's organization completely. But he couldn't just stuff them both into an oil drum. He'd never be taken seriously again. Even if they had managed to rape his favorite whore, it wasn't grounds for dumping them into the Ohio. Red would be watching to see how Bruno controlled his boys.

Shit. Now he was going to have to put off tonight's job. He needed Manny. Al was of no use to him—his kidneys weren't big enough.

———

LOGBOOK ENTRY:

I WAS STILL PONDERING Claudette's surprise invitation as Joey and I retraced our steps to the tailor's shop where the Cadillac was parked.

Joey said, "It's still too early to get your suit. What d'ya say we go back to the hospital—I need to check with my ma and see how Pop is doing."

I snapped him a salute. "Aye, aye, Captain."

We drove slowly in the heavy, end of the workday traffic. At a stop light, Joey glanced at me. "So, what do you think of Claudette? Now *there's* a woman for ya, Nicky boy." He wiggled his eyebrows at me. "She sure had eyes for you."

And I intended to take her up on that invitation.

Once we got to the hospital, I told Joey I'd stay out of his way and wait by the car. He didn't have any argument with that. I watched him disappear through the front entrance, and pulled out my pipe. I didn't want to go up there, mostly because I felt like I was barging in on personal family problems. But also because of Pearl. Just being around her confused me. I'd heard stories about guys my age having a roll in the hay with older women. But with your best pal's mom? Hell, maybe spending time with Claudette would straighten me out and get me through the next week.

I was tapping my pipe out on my shoe when Joey reappeared. His expression was serious.

"Situation's still the same," he said, as we got into the car. "My mom's a tough lady, but I'm sure glad my big sister's up there by her side. Look, we'll go home first. I'll change into my tux, then we'll pick up your stuff and get over to the club for dinner."

That's what we did. Except for the unscheduled stop at the police station Joey made between his getting dressed and me getting my suit at Saul's.

Inside, Joey marched up to the desk sergeant and demanded to speak to the detectives who were working on his father's case. Pope and Ducker were just signing out for the day. But they were accommodating and agreed to talk to Joey.

I knew my pal wasn't exactly Mister Diplomacy, but I was scratching my head over how hostile he was right from the get go. Joey launched his attack by telling Detectives Pope and Ducker the Cleveland Syndicate was responsible for shooting his father, and demanded to know what the hell they were going to do about it.

Pope was pretty patient, explaining to Joey about finding bullets and cartridge casings and sending them to the FBI for fingerprint analysis.

"That's all we can do right now," Pope said.

Joey wasn't satisfied. "That's it? Aren't you gonna go talk to your connections, beat the bushes, do something other than sit on your fat asses?" He was getting red in the face.

Detective Ducker answered, "Excuse me, *Mister* Jules. But who, exactly, should we be aiming this dragnet at?"

"You know damn well who I'm talking about—" Joey snapped back, "—that fucking Red Masterson. But you guys aren't gonna cross into that territory, nosirree—"

"Excuse my friend," I said to the detectives. I saw all too well where this was heading. "He's been under a lot of strain the last eighteen hours."

"Yeah, sure," replied Pope.

I heard Ducker mutter, "Strain, my ass."

Joey was about to open his mouth again. I nudged him. Hard. "Let's go."

Joey hesitated, but I used my size advantage to herd him out before he got himself arrested for disorderly conduct, or some such charge I could see forming in the brain of one Detective Ducker.

I hustled Joey down the street towards the Cadillac. Pushing him into the front seat from the curb side, I said, "The hell's the matter with you, Joey? What was all that about?"

"Fucking cops. They're not going to do anything about Pop. Sure, they get their gifts from us at Christmas time, but their stockings are stuffed big time by Cleveland. So, who do you think they're gonna back?"

"Okay, okay, but flying off the handle is just plain stupid."

Joey cursed and gripped the steering wheel like he had intentions of twisting it into a pretzel.

"Let me drive," I said. Didn't want to risk cutting short my furlough and spending the next six months in some hospital bed.

JOEY DIDN'T LET me drive, but he also didn't wrap us around any telephone poles on the way to Saul's. The suit fit fine. I had to rescue my old duds from the trash can Joey had thrown them in.

On the way to The Oasis, I resurrected my curiosity about the place—after all, it was the main reason I'd broken my promise to myself and come back to within spitting distance of my old man.

I'd been hearing Joey's stories about it for a while and figured he'd been exaggerating. But as soon as I saw that white dome breaking over the tree tops with THE OASIS in pink neon script, and we pulled into the parking lot filling up with Cadillacs, Lincolns, and Packards, it occurred to me the cocky bastard might have been telling the truth all along.

The place was damn big. A doorman greeted the customers driving up to the front entrance, and car jockeys whisked their automobiles around to the back lot. Joey took us to the back, too, and brought the Cadillac to a halt beside a door.

"Follow me," Joey said, getting out. He stopped and stared down at the gravel just outside the door. Noticing a patch that was darker than the rest, I wondered if it was the spot where Carl Jules had been gunned down.

I waited quietly as Joey lifted his head and looked out across the parking lot. He squinted as though looking for a ghostly image—an answer to what had happened the previous night.

Joey blinked, shook his head, and turned back to me, a brighter look on his face. "Okay, Nicky boy," he said, rubbing his hands together, "*Show* time."

As we walked past a DeSoto parked next to us, he thumped its hood. "This is the old clunker I was driving before you got here."

We went around to the front entrance, where the doorman greeted Joey with a handshake. "We're all pulling for your dad, Joe."

The foyer buzzed with anticipation. You'd think the patrons were going to the premiere of the latest Clark Gable movie. The ladies were all dolled up in sparkling gowns and the guys were decked out in tuxes or expensively tailored business suits. I was sure glad Joey had suited me up good and proper for the occasion.

The red carpeting and large glossy posters on the wall announcing the acts for that night added to the feeling I was in a movie palace, not some den of illegal gambling. The biggest poster showed a dapper-looking gent, gazing out at some distant point, with a knowing look in his eyes. He held his cigarette between sophisticated-looking fingers. Above the name Rudy Fitch, I read: *The Sensation of New York's Swank Spots.* I guessed he was the headliner.

"That's the lush," Joey said.

We checked our hats and I got a bright smile from the gal behind the counter, but it was obvious she had eyes for Joey.

"It's awful about your dad," she said. "Hope you catch whoever did it."

Joey nodded. "Thanks." He ignored the signals she was trying to send him with her eyes and, instead, he turned to me. "Let me give you the tour."

We moved from the foyer into the first room. In the center was a circular bar big enough to seat sixty people. Half the stools were already occupied and two bartenders were busy shaking cocktails. A lot of people were walking through an arched entryway that opened to another room behind the bar. In a Middle Eastern style of lettering above the door I read: CARAVAN ROOM.

"We'll be having dinner in there," Joey said, "but first I want to show you where the real action will be tonight." He led on past a large sweeping staircase. "That goes up to the offices."

Here and there I saw tough-looking fellows dressed in tuxedos just standing or strolling about by themselves, watching the customers. "Security," Joey said, when I asked about them. "See that guy over there?"

I looked in the direction he indicated and saw one of the tuxedoed security men staring out a window.

Joey said, "He's got one of the most important jobs in the whole joint. He's watching the headlights of a car parked across the road. The car jockeys take turns sitting in there. We're on a pretty big hill and Route 9 is the only road that comes up here directly from Newport. You can see anybody coming up that road long before they get here. So, if the car jockey on watch sees a couple of patrol cars, that's a good bet there's a raid on. He'll flash the headlights and our man inside will sound the alarm."

By then, we were entering a room filled with crap tables, blackjack tables, roulette wheels, and god knows how many slot machines. "What good does *that* do you?" I asked. "You'd only have what? Five minutes? How the hell do you hide all this stuff?"

"Three and a half minutes. Pop built this place especially with that in mind and everybody's got their job— they know the drill."

I looked around, imagining the commotion that must go on, and shrugged. "Guess it works. You're still in business."

From there, we went into the Caravan Room.

"We can seat about seven hundred for dinner," Joey said.

The room was filled with dining tables surrounding a highly-polished dance floor. On a stage, members of the dance band were getting their instruments ready. A banner with *The Sparkling Jules Review* spelled out in bright red letters stretched across the wall behind them. Doc Miller looked up from his music and waved hello to us as we walked onto the stage.

"Going to introduce my pal to the girls," Joey said.

After Joey turned to lead the way backstage, I caught a look of exasperation on Doc's face. He quickly covered it up with a smile when he realized I was watching.

The only time I'd seen the inside of a backstage dressing room was in a Busby Berkeley movie. This wasn't much different. It was as plain as a storage room, except for the beautiful half-naked women sitting at their line of makeup mirrors. They all turned and greeted Joey as we walked in. Everybody seemed happy to see him. Except for one knockout of a redhead who glared at him, then turned back to her mirror and attacked her face with a powder puff.

"Hi, girls," Joey said, putting his hand on my shoulder. "Want you to meet my pal Nick Cavanaugh. He's here with me on leave for the next week, so you all be nice to him. I don't wanna hear about any fights—there's plenty of him to go around."

I said, "Hi," and the gals all looked me up and down. A brunette, sitting at the end of the row of tables nearest us, whistled. "He's even bigger than Hunch and a lot better looking, that's for sure. I'm first in line." She turned to Joey, a sudden change of expression on her face. "It's terrible about your dad. We're praying for him. Hunch gathered everybody into the Caravan Room and told us what he knew."

One of the other gals added, "Hope Pearl comes back soon, we miss her already."

The band started to play some soft dinner music and Joey took it as his cue to get us out of the gals' hair so they could finish dressing for the show.

Joey seated me at a table, front row center, and said, "You order—I'll have the same. Be right back. Gotta make sure the lush isn't battling stage fright with a bottle."

Joey returned just as our dinners were being served. The lush was in good shape, and the steaks were great. Looking around, I saw a face I was more accustomed to seeing on a big movie screen. I watched the guy pay the cigarette girl for some smokes, and leaned across the table towards Joey. "Hey, isn't that Errol Flynn?"

Joey glanced over his shoulder. "Yep, that's him. He's been here before. Get a look at the babe he's with—can't be a day over seventeen. Lots of big shots show up here." He nodded at another table. "There's a judge. Behind him are a couple of radio executives from WLW in Cincinnati." Joey jabbed his thumb towards the gambling room. "They'll all be in there playing the tables after the show. If the Reds were playing a home game, you'd see a bunch of them here, too."

Suddenly, I realized the band was really swinging. I turned in my chair to watch one of the saxophone players, who'd stood up and launched into a solo. The guy didn't look like he had the strength to even lift the sax, never mind get much of a sound out of it. I said to Joey, "That fella's cookin'."

"Oh, yeah. That's 'Tweety'. His real name's Raymond Twitty, but he's got this real high voice and the rest of the band members kinda razz him. Nobody makes fun of his playing though."

After the waiter cleared away our plates, I ordered a bourbon and lit up my pipe. The Sparkling Jules Review started off with two male gymnasts flipping each other around the stage. After that, a big-chested lady in a glittering gown belted out a torch song. The audience thought the next act was funny. The setup was this guy and gal are dancing cheek-to-cheek in a Paris wine cellar, but they wind up bashing one another with everything on the stage, including a wine cask. Ha.

The headliner, Rudy "The Lush" Fitch looked sober, but sleazy. He sat down at the piano and spent the next twenty minutes singing songs with double entendres, all the while flashing knowing leers and toothy grins. Rudy went over big with the crowd, but to me the guy's act was as appetizing as a plate of fish heads. The finale was a hell of a lot better. All those leggy chorus gals, I'd met earlier, were paired up with eight guys for a big jitterbug number which brought the house down.

After the applause died, Joey said, "Let's get outta here. They play bingo in this room between shows. It's popular—draws in the low-risk taking customer." He got up from the table. "I don't think that's your game."

"You're right, I need something more exciting."

"We don't make much money off the bingo," Joey added. "In fact, the club donates what we take in to the various churches and synagogues in the area."

We joined a line of other like-minded patrons filing out a secondary exit and into a small lobby right in front of the gaming room. The line moved slowly, snaking between a set of double doors that looked sturdy enough to ward off an enemy attack. As I passed by one door, I grabbed hold of it and tried to give it a little swing. Damn, it was heavy. Must have been solid oak, at least three inches thick. I imagined the

Newport police racing up the road, and all the guys inside this castle on top of the hill scrambling into this room, slamming the doors and sliding a massive bar in place. I made a note to myself to start writing that adventure novel.

Once we were inside, Joey steered me to the money cage and told the cashier to give me fifty dollars in chips. "That'll get you into some of the games."

"Thanks. Maybe I'll try some blackjack."

"Good luck. I'll be walking around, checking on things."

Joey went towards the row of slot machines along the far wall and I headed for the tables. I was concentrating on the cards and didn't notice when the chorus girls appeared, until there was one standing by my arm.

"Told you I'd be first in line."

I looked into the face of the whistling brunette, then down at the rest of her. The gal had been poured into a strapless gown that showed off her curves. She looked great and she knew it.

Behind her, I could see the rest of the dancers, all dressed to kill and lingering around the other tables. I guessed it was part of their job to mix with the customers between shows.

I finished my hand, which won me my first couple of bucks—must have been the brunette who turned my luck around. I got to my feet to stretch my legs. "What's your name?"

"Sally," she answered, looking up at me. "And yes, I'll be your lucky charm for the rest of the night."

I looked into that adoring face again and was tempted to march over to the money cage and empty my wallet—if I had any money. I laughed to myself. *That's* why the dancers were out here. Lonely dentists from Toledo, coming over from their conventions in Cincinnati, wouldn't stand a chance against a temptation like this gal. Pretty slick.

Just then, I felt a slap on my back and turned. Joey said, "Break the bank yet?"

I was about to say no when I saw, over Joey's shoulder, the redheaded dancer with the knife-throwing eyes marching determinedly towards us. "Joey. Think you've got some trouble coming."

"Huh? What?" Joey turned to look behind him.

"You sonofabitch," the redhead said through clenched teeth, and tossed the contents of a glass she was carrying into Joey's face. Sally screeched. I got splashed, too, and a couple of ice cubes bounced onto the blackjack table.

Joey grabbed the redhead's wrist. "What the hell was that for, Ginnie?"

"'Cause you're a bastard. I saw you coming out of that whorehouse this afternoon."

Joey frowned. "What're you doing? Spying on me? I wasn't even doing anything in there."

"Oh, yeah. I suppose you weren't doing anything last night in the dealers' break room."

"Well—"

Ginnie lashed out with her foot, slamming him on the shin. "I hate you," she screamed.

Hunch appeared out of nowhere, and in a deep, low voice said, "Miss, you're fired."

Joey waved him away. "That won't be necessary." He grabbed Ginnie by the arm. "Calm down. Let's go talk about this." He led her out of the room, past the amused stares of some of the customers—most had already turned back to their gambling.

Hunch rubbed his temple and walked away. I might have been imagining it, but I could swear I heard him mutter, "Like father, like son."

I said to Sally, "He's only been home a few days. Didn't take him long to get into trouble."

"Those two were together before the war started. Only I think Ginnie took it more seriously than Joey did. She's been carrying a torch for him ever since he joined up." Sally leaned close towards me. "Mr. Jules, Joey's dad, never knew about it. Romances between employees are against the rules—and that includes Joey." She took my arm and snuggled up. "But that doesn't include you and me."

IT WAS TWO-THIRTY in the morning when we turned in the driveway of the Jules' house, Joey in the Cadillac and me in the DeSoto. It had been a fun night—I'd flirted with Sally, won a few bucks—but my body was demanding I put it to bed. I'd only had a couple hours of sleep over the last twenty-four.

Inside, Pearl greeted us from the top of the stairs. All she wore was a blue silk robe. Blond curls framed her face. Damn. In the dim hall lighting and from that distance, she could have been twenty years old and making a move on her wouldn't have been taboo.

"Hello, boys," Pearl said. "Everything go all right, tonight?"

Joey filled his mother in on how the night went—minus his run in with the chorus girl. "And how about Pop?" he asked.

"The same. I think. I stared at him for so long, I thought I saw him move. But it must have just been wishful thinking."

The pain in Pearl's voice made me feel like a real turd. She obviously was in love with her husband, and I had no business getting hot about her.

I didn't hear how the conversation ended, but the next thing I knew, Pearl was saying, "Good night, Nick."

I looked up and called out, "Good night, Mrs. Jules." But she'd already disappeared.

A little later, after saying good night to Joey, I was lying on my bed in the guest room with the door closed, staring up at the ceiling and listening to Pearl cry in her bedroom.

I heard Joey's door open. There were a couple of knocks. Then, "Mom?"

The crying stopped. Pearl answered, "Go away."

Joey's door closed, and all was quiet.

But not inside my head.

My mind's eye saw the knob on my bedroom door turn. Pearl walked into the room and stood beside my bed, looking down on me, a soft smile on her lips. She untied her belt, letting the silk robe fall from her shoulders. It slid down over her hips and fell to the floor. She had nothing on underneath. If she'd really been there, I'd have reached out and stroked the soft white skin of her breasts.

Dammit. Why is it I never get what I really want?

———

RAYMOND TWITTY GRABBED a pair of scissors and leaned out the window. On the rusted fire escape was his little flower garden—a row of clay pots filled with geraniums. He snipped a stem, heavy with pink flowers, and carried it over to a green painted dresser. Pearl looked back at him from all around the edges of its mirror. Raymond smiled at the photos, removed the faded flower from the crystal vase on top of the dresser, and replaced it with the fresh offering. He gazed at the photos, lingering for a moment over each one, then pulled out a pad of paper, a pen, and a bottle of ink from the top dresser drawer. Raymond filled his fountain pen and went to sit at the card table where he ate his meals.

In his careful but clumsy script, Raymond wrote:

My Dear Pearl,

How you must be suffering. As am I. I missed you so, these past two nights. My music is lifeless without you in the club—

"Aagh!" Raymond balled up the piece of paper and threw it on the floor. "That's shit." He rubbed his hand over his mouth. "Start again."

My Darling Pearl, . . .

12

10:00 A.M.

PEARL LEANED OVER CARL'S motionless body, stroked his bandaged forehead, and smoothed one of his unruly eyebrows. She kissed him on the lips. "Good morning, Carmelo. It's Pearlie."

She sat down on the chair next to the hospital bed. "God, please, I beg You. Bring him back today."

That's what Pearl woke up thinking, and she'd prayed it continually as she got dressed, slipped quietly out of the house so as not to disturb Joey and his friend Nick, got into the DeSoto and drove to the hospital.

Pearl rubbed her eyes. "I'm exhausted, Carmelo. I can't sleep in that bed by myself, wondering where you are. Can you hear me? Move a finger. Twitch. *Something.*"

She waited, scanning his body for the slightest movement.

There was nothing.

"The club is still open. Hunch and Doc are keeping it going. Joey was there last night, too. Our son's a good boy, Carmelo. And Lauretta's trying to help. But I can't take comfort from anyone. Nothing's going to make me feel better until you come back."

Pearl reached for the gold crucifix hanging around her neck, and rubbed it between her thumb and fingers. Of all the presents Carl had showered her with over the years, this crucifix had always remained her favorite. He'd given it to her when Lauretta was born.

"I don't know what I'd do without you." She shook her head. "I'm sorry. No, I can't think that way—like you say, 'we'll keep going, there could be a miracle just around the corner.'"

Pearl held Carl's thickly stubbled face in her hands and stared at his closed eyes, trying to will them open. "Come on, Carmelo. I'll sing the song.

Ev'ry time it rains,
It rains pennies from heaven.
Don't you know each cloud contains
Pennies from heaven.
You'll find your fortunes—"

Pearl started to sob.

"No! I told myself I wasn't going to cry." She pulled a handkerchief out of her purse and dabbed at her eyes. "They

125

haven't beaten us yet, Carmelo. But I'm worried about Joey. You know how he is—he got it from me. I saw the letter you had in your pocket, and so did Joey. Now that they've done this to you, I don't know how I'm going to hold him back."

Pearl looked across the room and out the window. "Carmelo, you and I know this is not just business. It's personal. And it'll always be that way with Jimmy the Shiv."

———

THE BLACK VOID surrounded Carl. He heard a familiar voice calling to him far in the distance, but he couldn't make out what it was saying. His head would not obey his commands to turn towards the voice.

Carl tried to wave his arms and shout *"Over here!"* but he felt disconnected from his body—all he could do was listen.

The voice kept talking. At first, it was garbled, but after a time a word here and there became recognizable. Carl heard his name. It was Pearl. *Thank God. Somehow she found me—she's coming to get me.* He tried to shout, *Pearlie,* but he couldn't make a sound.

She was singing.

Pearlie. He tried to force her name through his lips.

The tune she sang was familiar. But her voice was muffled, like she was in another room. Carl heard "You'll find your fortunes—" Then she started to cry.

Why was she crying? *It's not a sad song.*

Pearl stopped, as if she'd heard him, then started talking again, her voice still muffled and far away.

Carl heard the name "Joey", then something about a letter and "they've done this to you."

Suddenly, the muffled words came through in complete sentences. "Carmelo, you and I know this is not just business. It's personal. And it'll always be that way with Jimmy the Shiv."

Jimmy the Shiv? No—

The glare of headlights shone through the black void. Carl remembered squinting into the lights as he stepped out the back door of the club. There were gunshots.

The next instant, Carl was driving his Lincoln, fully loaded with crates of whiskey, over the rutted road outside Bellaire, Ohio, on his run from Cincinnati to Pittsburgh. He looked in his rear view mirror and squinted in the glare of the reflected headlights. His partner, Jimmy Turelli, was right behind him. Shots rang out. Carl stepped on the gas pedal. Almost every time he and Jimmy hit this dark, hilly stretch of their route, someone would try to stop them. He never did find out whether it was bandits or the local police, hoping to get paid off with a couple of cases of "the good stuff", because they never succeeded.

Carl pushed the Lincoln to its limit, anticipating every turn and twist in the road. Both he and Jimmy could drive this route blindfolded, they'd done it so many times. That's why George Remus had made them part of his gang.

No. It wasn't Jimmy the Shiv who shot him. It didn't make sense. Jimmy could have plugged him more than twenty years earlier during any one of those runs and no one would've asked questions.

Why would he wait until now?

———

STEVE POPE WAS at his desk at the police station, bright and early, though he had endured another sleepless night. He'd spent the whole time lying in bed, staring up at the ceiling and remembering the pain of Sister Mary Alfred's ruler whacks as she tried to pound the difference between mortal and venial sins into his ten-year-old knuckles. Pope had carried on a phantom argument with her all night long, taking the side that accepting bribes—which hurt nobody—was a venial sin, easily absolved in the confessional. He didn't convince Sister Mary Alfred.

He picked up the coroner's report on Charlie "The Dandy" DePalma, and was reading it when Ducker came in with coffee and donuts. The short of it was Dandy Charlie didn't drown—he suffocated.

Pope said to Ducker, "Guess that drum was sealed pretty tight, until the barge accident." He leafed through DePalma's file. "So that's it, huh? No next of kin. No one to notify. The end of a life and nobody cares."

Ducker grunted as he settled into his chair.

"But the guy had some function in Masterson's crowd," Pope said, setting the file back down on his desk. "He's gotta be replaced by someone."

Ducker munched on a donut. "Yeah. I guess."

"So, whoever's taken over is the one who rubbed him out, or at least knows who did. Who's collecting now for Red Masterson?"

"Who cares? Cuz, why're you sniffing around that fire hydrant again?"

"Just asking." Pope picked up a second file. "Well, you can't say nobody cares about Mr. Jules."

Ducker swung his feet off his desk. "No, shit. I was

ready to throw that kid of his into the lockup to cool down, yesterday. Good thing his buddy pushed him out. That's a *big* guy. He must be at least six-three or four."

"You can't blame the kid for getting emotional over what happened to his dad."

"I'm getting sick and tired of these goddamn plain ol' greasy donuts. I'm gonna tell that deli where they can get some decent black market chocolate."

"Stop kidding around. I'm serious."

"So am I. Swiss chocolate, too."

"Look. What can we do about this shooting? We won't get the results of the fingerprint test for a few weeks. We've seen one of those nine millimeter CORTOs before. Didn't they dig one out from a hired gun who went up against Red Masterson a few years ago when Pete Schmidt tried to fight back against Cleveland?"

"Yeah. I remember that. It was a Beretta."

"So, wouldn't you say it's logical to speculate this could be the same situation and that Carl's boy is right about Cleveland?"

Ducker shrugged.

"If the gun turns out to be an Italian-made automatic, the only guys around this area who'd be able to get their hands on it would be Red Masterson's people. Or some of the other well-connected independent casino operators like Sleepout Louie Levinson."

Ducker waved his hand. "Hey, hey, you forgetting Carl Jules, himself? He's a member of that club, too. And don't forget, he was wearing a shoulder holster, but we never did find *his* piece."

He stood up, came around to Pope's desk, and sat on

the edge of it. "Shit, looks like he could've been shot with his own gun." He tapped the Jules file with a greasy forefinger. "I still say there's a good chance the wife did it. Said she was home sick that night. Alone."

Ducker leaned forward and slowly shook his head in Pope's face. "And there ain't nobody there to vouch for her."

13

I WOKE UP WITH A start from a deep sleep and, once again, it took me a few seconds to work through my confusion and remember where I was.

I pulled on my pants, opened my bedroom door and shuffled into the corridor. Joey's snores practically shook the door of his room, but the door to Pearl's was open. Her bed was made and the room was empty. On my way to the head, I stopped at the top of the stairs and listened, but there were no sounds of activity below.

After I finished my business, I returned to my room

and sat at the desk to record the previous day's events in my logbook. When I got to the part about my fantasy with Pearl, I hesitated. Did I really want to put that down in black and white? Shit, I was going to have to do something about the way I felt before I lost whatever bit of common sense I possessed and did something really stupid.

How was I going to get through the next week? Whatever I did to fill up my time, it had to be something that I could pour all my energy into. I leaned back in the chair, looked up, and there, mounted on the wall right in front of me, was my answer. The rows of Joey's books and his stack of pulp magazines smacked me right between the eyes. Here I was, living right in the middle of a *Spicy Detective* story.

I grabbed the magazines off the shelf, and shuffled through the stack. Yep. There was a *Spicy Detective*—half-naked babe on the cover fighting off her gun-toting attacker. I flipped through the "full length novel" inside. Hell, I could write as good a story as *Two Hands To Choke*. In fact, I had already started the story just with what I'd put into my logbook the last couple of days.

What I needed was to find out more about this place—but without people knowing why I was nosing around. Had to be careful, otherwise everybody would clam up.

My mind was suddenly buzzing with ideas. For the next half hour I wrote furiously in my book, trying to keep up, until the clatter of pots and pans downstairs broke my concentration. Flora the housekeeper must have arrived. I was starving, so I threw on my shirt and moseyed on down to the kitchen.

I was drinking a glass of orange juice Flora handed me, and reading the newspaper—Nazi troops were pouring into southern Italy, and Dick Tracy was hot on Mrs. Pruneface's trail—when Joey rolled in, yawning and scratching the back of his neck.

Flora poured another glass of juice and set it down on the table for Joey. "Found this on the counter, Mr. Joe," she said, handing him a note. "Sez your mama's gone off to the hospital."

Joey took a look out the side kitchen window. "Great, she left us the Cadillac." He turned back to me. "What should we do today? I've gotta go back to the hospital, but what would you like to do?"

"I think I should get outta your hair for a while, let you take care of your mom. Drop me off downtown and I'll just wander around, kill some time, go pick up my sports jacket. I'll meet you over at the club for dinner."

"That's a lotta time to kill—ain't that much to see around here. Less, of course, you take Claudette up on her invite."

Yeah. "I could."

"You should." Joey picked up his glass of juice and threw it back like it was a shot of tequila. "Might need a rest after that. Know what? Go over to the hotel—Lauretta'll let you put your feet up in the lobby."

"What hotel? The Glenn Hotel?"

"Naw. The Joseph—named after me—I told you about it. My sister runs the place."

Joey'd never mentioned it, but I wasn't going to get into an argument about it. I just asked, "What's the address?"

"Corner of Third and Monmouth."

ON THE WAY to Newport, I asked Joey if he'd patched things up with his girl friend or if the dancer was out of a job.

He rolled his eyes, but kept them trained on the road ahead. "Dancers are high-strung babes, but I think I managed to talk some sense into her. Didn't want to see the gal get fired because of that scene last night. Anyway, Ginnie's not my girl friend." He flashed a smile at me. "You know I'm not gonna get tied down—there's too many fish in the sea."

Joey turned his attention back to the traffic and we rode in silence for a minute. I changed the subject and asked Joey why a hotel was named after him. Expecting some wise crack response, I was surprised when I got a straight answer. He explained it was an old hotel, built before the turn of the century, and bragged it was a place where Al Capone and other gangsters would hole up while the heat was on back in the early Twenties. About 1930, it became the first piece of property Carl Jules bought in Newport and since Joey was his first son, it was renamed in his honor.

The Joseph Hotel sounded like a place that had some stories to tell, so I figured its lobby might offer something more than a place to put up my feet. I'd stroll over there after visiting Saul's Tailoring.

Joey dropped me off at Saul's and pointed north. "The Joseph Hotel's a short walk up towards the river."

"See you tonight at the club," I said, as Joey drove off.

Saul greeted me like I was an old pal. I tried on my new sports jacket and trousers—looked sharp. "Wrap these up," I said, handing my old duds over to Saul. In the back of my mind, I was thinking about how I'd look to Claudette if I visited her later.

Walking up Monmouth Street was a different

experience, now that I was on my own. The even rows of two-story brown and gray brick storefronts had a tired, worn look. Didn't appear that any new buildings had gone up in Newport for the past twenty years. Even so, her sidewalks were bustling with the mid-day activity of shoppers, truckers dropping off deliveries, and workers heading for an early lunch.

But what I noticed the most was the bad taste in my mouth and the difficulty I had breathing. On my previous trip along this street, the distraction of talking to Joey, meeting new people and saving a prostitute from getting raped kept me from noticing how gritty and stench-filled the air was. Figured it was coming from the steel mills or across the river from Cincinnati. Whatever the source, it stung my eyes and tasted awful. The gas fumes from the constant stream of cars and trucks and buses didn't help much, either.

The Joseph Hotel was easy to spot—it was a three-story brown brick building, its entrance just around the corner on Third Street. Calling it a hotel was stretching it. It was more of a flophouse than a Waldorf Astoria. But it was a clean flophouse.

The lobby was large enough to hold two slightly worn sofas, four green leather armchairs, and a big, potted palm. I recognized Lauretta behind a small counter that had a hand-lettered sign instructing guests to SIGN IN HERE.

She looked up as soon as I walked in. I knew she recognized me right away because her eyes widened with surprise, but she still waited for me to walk up to the counter and reintroduce myself. "Nick Cavanaugh," I said. "Joey's friend?"

"Hi," she said in a shy voice. "Can I help you with something?"

We were off to an awkward start. I told her I was just walking around town and Joey'd suggested I drop by for a visit. I started asking her a couple of questions about the hotel's history, but she stopped me and said, "I'm not much on history. You want to talk to Gabby. He's an older gentleman, mostly hangs around the lobby and every now and then helps my husband Mike—"

"*Bang!Bang!Pow!*"

I turned towards the sound. There was another series of high-pitched *Bang!Bang!Pows!* My attacker popped out from behind one of the green leather chairs. The little squirt was wearing a cowboy hat and toting a wooden rifle.

"Victor Lloyd. You march over here, young man," Lauretta said, the tone of her voice turning sharp. There was a drill sergeant lurking inside that mouse. The little desperado obeyed, and Lauretta proceeded to give him a dressing-down.

To me, she said, "You must excuse me, but I hate that gun. I seem to be the only one in this family that sees anything wrong with it. But his Uncle Joey gave it to him for his birthday, so I can't take it away from him. Joey thinks guns make great presents. I don't. Best I can do is teach my boy not to point it at people."

"No harm done," I said, "he's just a kid."

"Well, there's too many guns out there. Seems like everybody around here carries one." Lauretta looked down at the counter, the mousiness returning to her voice. "Sorry... All this business with my father getting shot... It's been..."

"No need to explain."

I found myself staring at her. With her head down and golden curls falling to her shoulders, the resemblance between momma and daughter was striking. "So where do I find this Gabby?"

Lauretta lifted her head to look at me. "Probably out back. He's supposed to be sweeping up—some critter got into the garbage." She tilted her head. "We live back here, but there's a hallway that'll take you to a back door."

She pointed down the corridor that ran beside the staircase.

I said, "Thanks, see you later," and found my way to the back of the hotel.

Outside, an old guy leaned on a broom, licking and sealing a hand rolled cigarette.

"Your name Gabby?" I asked.

"Yep. Who's askin'?"

I introduced myself and my connection to Joey Jules, then told him I'd heard he was a good source of stories from "the old days." Gabby lived up to his name.

I pulled out my pipe and lit up as he filled me in on the Remus Gang business that Pete Schmidt had mentioned the day before in his rant to Joey and me. Seems Schmidt wasn't exaggerating. He and Carl Jules and this guy I kept hearing about, Red Masterson, along with a bunch of others, had been part of an extremely smart and elaborate operation.

Gabby said, "George Remus was called 'King of the Bootleggers'. Lived in a big mansion over on the Cincinnati side of the river. That guy had brains—used to be a pharmacist, then became a lawyer up in Chicago. Defended all kinds of murderers and bootleggers. The story goes, Remus saw how much money those dumb bastards were making with the booze, so he packed up his law books and moved down here. This was the center of the liquor business."

Gabby pulled out his tobacco pouch and kept talking as he rolled up another fat cigarette. "Now Remus was a cagey fella—knew how to work around the law. In those days, the only legal way you could get your hands on bonded whiskey was if you was making medicine or hair tonic. So, you remember I told you he was a pharmacist? He goes and buys up these drug companies—even sets up new ones—then he goes and buys up warehouses full of liquor, gets all the permits and runs the liquor through the drug companies and out into the bootleg market."

Gabby slapped his knee and chuckled. "His gang trucked that stuff all over the country. Old George sure was a character. Even after the Feds put him away in the pen, he was running his operation from his jail cell. Word had it, he even had a maid keeping his cell all nice and neat for him.

"Yessiree. This place was full of characters in the good ol' days. You had Bob Zwick, they called him 'the Fox of Gangland'. He was a hijacker, a hired gun. Him and his girl friend Dago Rose lived over at the Glenn Hotel. Zwick hung out in the lobby carrying his submachine gun. Then there was that guy who took part in the St. Valentine's Day Massacre up in Chicago. What was his name? Oh, yeah. Dave Jerus—called him 'Jew Bates' around here."

I guess I had a look of disbelief, because Gabby nodded his head violently and said, "Oh, yeah. Little Mexico was a wild place. You'd see guys walking up and down the street with their tommy guns slung over their shoulders. Once in a while there were shoot-outs, but for the most part they stayed quiet 'cause they were running from the law in other states. Outlaws knew they weren't gonna be bothered here. Stayed at the Glenn—some here at the Joseph. Things have quietened down even more since then. On account of Red 'the Enforcer' Masterson. He's kinda the unofficial sheriff of Little Mexico—works for the Cleveland boys who own most of the flashy casinos here. They don't want trouble from any hoods. Killings and holdups ain't good—scares away the convention business from Cincinnati. So Red's job is to roam around town, making sure that stuff don't happen."

I raised my pipe for a question. "Why they call Newport 'Little Mexico'?"

Gabby jerked his thumb south. "You seen those hills down there? Think those roads are bad now? Back then they were almost impassable. Long as outlaws keep to this little corner of Northern Kentucky here and stay outta the rest of the state, those officials down in Frankfort ignore us. And over that way," his thumb pointed north, "is a whole other state. They can't do nothing about us. This area's a hideout. You know—like the Old West. Outlaws'd cross the Rio Grande and hole up in Mexico. Same thing here."

This was all entertaining stuff, but I wanted to ask him about Carl Jules without sounding like I was some news hound doing an article for *The Kentucky Times-Star*. Didn't want this source of information to suddenly dry up because of loyalty to the Jules family.

I said, "Heard Joey's dad was driving for Remus, too, but he never got caught."

"Yep. 'Lucky' Jules. Those other guys like Pete Schmidt, Red Masterson, Jimmy 'the Shiv' Turelli—they all did time."

I remembered the hostile look on Schmidt's face when he uttered the name Lucky Jules. I asked Gabby what I thought was a natural question. "Think they were steamed at him?"

"Probably."

"Still?"

"Ya never can tell. Some of those guys are part Eye-talian, and wops can hold on to a grudge tighter than a coon dog'll hold on to his last bone."

14

CLAUDETTE SAT IN FRONT of her vanity mirror, playing the role of Ingrid Bergman's Ivy the barmaid to Spencer Tracy's Mr. Hyde. She'd just come back from the matinee showing of *Dr. Jekyll and Mr. Hyde* at the State Theater, convinced she could do a better job. After all, acting was nothing more than memorizing your lines and digging down deep inside to feel what it's like to say them. She pictured Bruno's ugly mug. Now *there* was a real life monster.

Claudette backed away from the mirror, her good side towards the "camera", eyes bulging as Mr. Bruno Hyde approached. She brought her hands up in front of her face, her tiny palms desperately trying to ward away the monster.

She waited a beat. Then screamed.

"Claudette?" Sophie's voice broke the dramatic spell.

Claudette smiled with satisfaction, as if the director had shouted, "Cut. Print it." Yep. She was good.

She went out into the hallway, to the top of the stairs. Sophie was standing at the bottom, speaking to someone hidden from view. Claudette heard her say, "It's all right, she's just come back from the movies."

Sophie turned and called up the stairs, "Claudette, you have a visitor."

Good. He's come. Claudette patted her hair, checked the seams on her stockings, and went downstairs. *What was his name again?* Shit, she'd forgotten. "Sophie, get lost. Well, hello there," Claudette said, extending her hand. Sailor Boy looked pretty sharp—new sports coat and slacks, polished shoes, expensive Panama. *The guy's got style. Big shoulders, too.*

Just as he took her hand, she remembered Joey's joke. Mister In-the-Nick-of-Time himself. "Swell of you to visit, Nick."

"Well, I had some things to do nearby, so I decided to stroll on over and see how you were—I mean, after what happened yesterday."

Still holding his hand, Claudette looked up at Nick. "Well, I've been in worse situations, but thanks. It's good you and Joey were there." She pulled him towards the velvet sofa in the parlor.

"Let's sit down," she said, keeping her eyes locked on his. "Did you know I read palms?"

"Joey told me you read minds."

"Oh? What else did Joey tell you about me?"

"That you were the one gal in Newport I had to meet."

Claudette pictured The Fool card popping out of her Tarot deck. "Do you believe in destiny?"

Big Sailor shrugged his shoulders. "Maybe. But I think you make your own luck, good or bad."

"Have you ever had your palm read?"

"Yep, once. In Spain. Only, she was an old gypsy. Ugly looking. You know, hooked nose, missing teeth."

Claudette looked at his hand, spread it out and ran her fingers lightly over the callouses on his palm. It was a very interesting hand.

He smiled down at her. "I suppose you're gonna tell me I work with my hands."

The remark irritated Claudette, but she smiled back. "No. As a matter of fact, your hand tells me you are a creative person. A thinker." She followed the trail of his heart line. "You have some major breaks here. Not so good with relationships, huh? Maybe your family?" Claudette looked up and thought she saw the confidence in his eyes desert him— but only for a moment.

"Oh, yeah? What else do you see?"

"You want to keep moving—you've got to. See how this line curves way out across your palm? That's your life line. It tells me you've got wanderlust. But I sense you're also a very ambitious man with a lot of dreams." *Just like me.*

Claudette felt certain this was the person the card predicted would come into her life. But the card didn't say *when* she'd get out of Newport, just to watch for opportunity. She caressed the palm of his hand. The guy was just a sailor—

what could he do for her? But The Fool pointed to an independent and unconventional person who'd appear out of nowhere. This sailor could fit the bill.

Claudette looked into Nick's eyes. "How does *that* compare to your old gypsy in Spain?"

"I like yours better." Nick leaned forward. "But are you sure Joey didn't tell you all about me?"

"Hmm. Believe me, when Joey was here earlier this week, you weren't the topic of our conversation."

"What about my love life?"

Claudette rolled up his fingers, into his palm. "It will be very adventurous. Let's go upstairs." She led him out of the parlor, but they had to wait at the bottom of the stairs while several of the other hookers filed down, giggling over some private joke.

Sophie came out of the kitchen at the back of the house and gave Claudette a look. Claudette knew what that look was all about. Every other day, Sophie would tell her girls, "You can do what you want on your own time, but if I was a dentist and pulled teeth all day, I wouldn't come home and yank a couple more molars just for kicks."

As Claudette led Nick up the stairs, she called out to Sophie, "We're going to play dentist."

CLAUDETTE WATCHED NICK set his hat down on a chair in her room, take off his jacket and hang it on the back, and move to her bed. She was a little surprised. Most first time visitors just stood there, shifting from one foot to the other, waiting for instructions. Seemed this sailor was used to making himself at home in strange surroundings. Claudette went to her vanity and ran a comb through her hair, and watched him in the mirror as he took off his shoes. He stretched out on the bed, leaned back against the headboard, and watched her.

Claudette started to unbutton the top of her dress. "No, not yet," Nick said. "Come here."

As she went over to the bed, he patted the mattress. "Lie here beside me."

It felt strange to Claudette, not being the one calling the shots, but she did as he said.

He kissed her on the neck and picked up where she'd left off, slowly undoing the row of buttons down the front of her dress. As his hand slid in under the top of her dress and pushed it off her shoulder, Claudette started to feel excited. Nick's touch was different from the scores of hands that had traveled across her body over the last three years. It was a caress, not a grope. Nick kissed the top of her shoulder as he pulled down the other side of her dress. She helped him, shaking her arms free of the sleeves.

"Hmm, you smell great," Nick said, into her neck. He kissed behind her ear, on her other shoulder, and in the hollow of her throat.

Claudette pulled his shirt out from his trousers and quickly unbuttoned it. *No undershirt—just like Clark Gable.* The hairs on his chest had a warm smell. She listened to the heart thumping inside, then raised her chin to meet his lips. What am I doing? she thought, looking at Nick through half-closed eyes. I don't let men kiss me on the lips. But this was different—he wasn't just another john. Nick might be The Fool who'd get her out of Newport.

As their lips touched, she remembered the warning: *Beware of The Fool. He is a challenge to tread warily.*

Claudette closed her eyes and parted her lips, letting his kiss deepen and his hands explore for ways to give her pleasure.

———

RAYMOND TWITTY FINISHED shaving the wispy hairs that grew on his face, and slapped on the *Aqua Velva*. He checked the clock again. It was only five. Too early to put on his suit.

His old jalopy had conked out on him again, and he'd had to call one of the other band members for a ride to work. But there were still two hours to kill before he had to be down at the corner to meet him.

"God, I hate this," he said out loud to the mirror. Then he practiced saying her name. "Pearl." He leaned closer to the mirror and watched himself say it again. "Pearl."

Raymond rubbed his sweating palms together and walked out of the bathroom, over to the saxophone case on the floor by his bed. He unclasped the case, pulled out a new reed, and stuck it in his mouth.

You've got to be there tonight, Pearl.

Tonight was the night he wanted to tell her. But he was afraid his tongue would trip him up, like it always did.

Raymond sucked noisily on the reed. He had no problem standing up on the bandstand in front of hundreds of people and baring his soul. He could express all his longings through music. Why couldn't he do it with words? Say it straight out so she'd know all that passion was for her. Now that Carl was gone—no, Raymond corrected himself, he

146

wasn't. The damn guy was still hanging on. Why? Carl wasn't going to be of use to anybody—especially Pearl. Poor, sweet Pearl. She was going to need someone to satisfy her needs. Raymond had seen the way she'd looked at him. She felt the same way he did about her. He knew it.

Why didn't he just grab her in his arms and pull her to him and kiss those perfect red lips? She had the sexiest mouth. He'd see her standing behind the bar, freshening up her red lipstick and wonder what those lips tasted like.

No, the caveman act wouldn't work on her. She appreciated intelligence and knew he wasn't like the rest of those greasy-haired goons in the band. They could make fun of him all they wanted. He didn't care. Raymond laughed. In fact, the more abuse they heaped on him, the better he'd look to Pearl. She'd seen how he stood up to them, and she admired his strength. He was sure of it.

But what could he say to her? Maybe writing it out first would help—memorize it like he would a piece of music. Raymond picked up one of the balls of crumpled paper from off the floor, and flattened it out on the card table. He sat down and skimmed over the words he'd written earlier. *Infantile blathering.* He flipped the page over. Start fresh. The apartment was silent except for the noise Raymond made sucking on his reed.

He pictured himself in his white tuxedo, suave and confident, holding Pearl's hand. He'd look into her blue eyes and say, "We don't need to keep our feelings hidden from each other anymore. I'm here for you. You are—" He spit out his reed. *"Oh, fuck! Fuck! Fuck!"*

Raymond shot to his feet, tearing the crumpled page into shreds. He kicked back the chair, then picked up the card table and flung it across the room, smashing it against the wall.

Raymond stomped back and forth through the tiny apartment, cursing and pounding at the air with his fists.

———

"YOU BETTER GET out of bed or you're gonna be late for work." Vera pulled the covers off Ginnie. "It's almost five o'clock. What's the matter with you?"

Ginnie grabbed the bed sheet and pulled it back. "Leave me alone. I'm not going."

"Wha—? You sick or something?"

"No."

"Then what's all this talk about The Oasis being so important to you that you'll go to your grave dancing on that stage?"

"Go away." Ginnie pulled the sheet over her head, and kept it there until she heard Vera leave and close the bedroom door behind her. She rolled the sheet back down and stared at the ceiling. Joey's talk last night had done nothing to calm her down, it just showed her how much of a bastard he was. Maybe he was right. Maybe she *had* wasted her time waiting for him.

If this goddam war hadn't happened, they'd probably be married by now. But being away changed him. All this talk about it being "unstable times" and "not making commitments" and "needing his freedom".

"Well, I'll show him I got my freedom, too."

Ginnie reached down under her bed, pulled out a fifth, and had a swig of breakfast.

"**H**EY, HAMBURGER FACE," Bruno said to Manny. "You screw up tonight, and the rest of your body's gonna match that mug of yours."

Bruno had just sauntered into the Yorkshire Club and got a look at his two stooges sitting at the bar. Neither Manny nor Al could look him in the eye.

"Okay. Tonight we're gonna try it again. We're paying a visit to The Oasis just like I told Red we were going to *last* night." Bruno pointed a finger at Manny. "I covered for you. Told Red I'd switched it to tonight 'cause it's a busier night and we want a big audience. But you screw up again, you gotta talk to Red yourself."

The bartender came over to the trio, holding an empty pitcher. "You guys want your water now?"

"Oh . . ." Bruno looked at his watch. "Give us another forty-five minutes. In the meantime, gimme a scotch."

"What about you guys?" the bartender asked Manny and Al.

"Nothing for them," Bruno said, wiping the air with his hand.

The bartender shrugged, poured the scotch, then went back to the sink and started filling pitchers with water.

15

LOGBOOK ENTRY:

I WAS GENTLY NUDGED out of Claudette's bedroom because it was almost seven P.M., opening time. Paying customers would be showing up soon.

Joey was right. Claudette was special—every sailor's fantasy. I'd been with all kinds of whores before, but it was hard to attach that tag to her. She was a real expert when it came to knowing how to make a guy feel good, even taught me a few things. But we'd spent the last hour lying in her bed, eating sandwiches, drinking a couple of beers and having a few laughs. It was more like having a picnic with an old girl friend.

I went down to the corner on Monmouth, saw a cab and hailed it. Told the driver I was going to The Oasis.

"You in a big rush?" The cabbie asked.

"No," I said, getting in. "Just don't take me the long way round—I've already seen the neighborhood."

"Hey, I wouldn't do that to you, buddy. I just gotta make a delivery over on York. Only take a minute or two. I won't start the meter until we get back up here. Deal?"

"Sure."

As we headed over to York Street, the cabbie tossed a look over his shoulder at me. "I'd never mess with anyone going to The Oasis. No cabbie would. Word got back to Carl Jules or Pearl and that driver'd be out on his ass. The cab companies around here do half their business shuttling people and packages around to the clubs. Can't afford to have any ill will, so to speak."

The cabbie turned onto a side street and looked at me in his rear view mirror. "I guess you read about what happened to Carl Jules? Damn shame, nice guy like that. Always the gentleman."

"His son's a pal of mine. I'm staying at their house."

The cabbie took another good look at me in his mirror. This time I saw a touch of nervousness in his eyes. "I—I'll get you there in a jiff. Here we are." He pulled up right in front of the Flamingo club and jumped out with a manila envelope. "Be right back."

Watching the cabbie hustle into the club with his mysterious little package sent my imagination off into working out the opening lines for a *Black Mask* story. I hadn't even spent two days in Little Mexico and I'd learned to suspect everybody was running some kind of racket.

Well, not *every*body.

But you just couldn't be sure. At that moment, I looked across the street and saw one of the band members from The Oasis in his white tuxedo standing on the corner, holding a large instrument case. It was the runty saxophone player. The one who could really play—Tweety.

Another guy was standing there with him. A big, hulking fella wearing a nice suit and an impressive scar down his left cheek. Looked kind of familiar, but I couldn't say why. He turned his back to me, and put his arm around Tweety's shoulder, like they were pals going over some last minute plans. I mentally changed the saxophone in Tweety's case into a tommy gun and was launching into an imaginary discussion about who was going to be hit that night, when the cabbie slid back into the driver's seat.

"Thanks for waiting, pal. Next stop, The Oasis."

It WAS A BIGGER crowd than the night before. I remarked to Joey, "Looks like it's gonna be a busy night."

He shrugged. "Good size."

Hunch Williams nodded a quiet hello to me. I nodded back. Guess that made us old pals.

I perched on a stool at the bar and watched Joey go to work. He looked like a natural, strutting around the club, greeting the customers and handing out orders to his staff. It was obvious Casino Boss was what he wanted to be after the war. He made his rounds and came over to the bar. After a short discussion with the bartender about the liquor inventory,

Joey asked him, with a tilt of his head in my direction, "You taking care of my friend?"

I said, "I don't need anything to drink right now, just finished off a few beers before coming here."

"Oh, yeah? Don't tell me you spent the whole afternoon sitting in somebody else's bar."

"Nope. I was drinking Claudette's beer."

Joey slapped me on the back. "Ha!"

"I'm hungry though."

"I bet you are. Go over to the table we sat at last night—that's ours—and I'll have some food sent over."

"Thanks. How's your dad?"

Joey stared down at the bar, gripped the edge with both hands, and dug his fingernails into the wood. "He ain't coming out of this." He clamped his lips tight and slowly shook his head.

I pictured Pearl sitting at Carl's bedside and wanted to ask how she was holding up, but I held my tongue, afraid my face or my tone of voice would expose more than just casual interest.

B Y THE TIME I'd finished my meal, the Caravan Room was filled to capacity and the Sparkling Jules Review was ready to roll again. It was the same show I'd seen the night before, except Tweety's hot saxophone solo was a few degrees cooler, and the chorus line was almost derailed when that redhead, Ginnie, caught my eye, winked at me and slammed into Sally, the dancer next to her, almost knocking off the poor girl's headdress.

I still didn't understand what made Rudy "The Lush" Fitch the *Sensation of New York.*

I also didn't understand the appeal of the after-the-show bingo game, so I left the table and moved with a good portion of the male half of the dinner crowd into the casino area. The fifty bucks Joey had grubstaked me were still in my pocket, so I traded them in for chips at the cashier cage, then headed to the roulette tables.

I caught sight of Joey standing at the row of slot machines on the other side of the room. He was busy explaining the intricate strategies for playing the one-armed bandits to a couple of matrons in sparkling gowns. Joey saw me watching and flicked me a salute. He said a few parting words that won him radiant smiles from the two old gals before they turned their attention to their new-found pastime and began feeding the hungry monsters.

"A couple of bankers' wives from Cincinnati," Joey explained, when he joined me at the roulette table. He watched me play a few spins of the wheel and lose each time.

"This table's not for me," I said, as I watched my bet get scooped away.

Joey shrugged. "Hang in there for a while, I'll cover you."

As I placed another bet, I spied Joey's redheaded dancer, dressed in a sexy gown, moving purposefully towards us. She looked a little unsteady on her feet, but seemed so determined, I quickly checked to see if she was carrying a glass of something wet to toss.

She wasn't. "Hi, Nick," she said, tossing herself at me. "Name's Ginnie. Remember me?"

"How could I forget?" I replied, glancing over her shoulder and catching Joey's look of surprise.

Joey's girl friend pressed herself up against me so I

could feel her breast squeezing against my arm. "I saw you out front tonight," she said.

"Yeah? I saw you, too."

"Buy me a drink?"

"I don't think you need one, Ginnie."

She gazed up into my face. "You're a really big guy. I like big guys."

I tried to throw a nonverbal *SOS* to Joey, but he was ignoring the both of us and playing my bet at the roulette table.

Ginnie turned, saw that Joey wasn't paying any attention, and frowned. I knew the game *she* was playing.

Just then, Hunch Williams showed up at the table and whispered into Joey's ear. Whatever Hunch told him was important—*damn* important. It was more important than the spinning roulette wheel, Ginnie, or me.

Joey spat out *"Dingdonging?"* and a string of curses under his breath, pushed past his security chief and marched out of the room. I followed, a step behind Hunch.

We ended up in the foyer. Every security guy on the payroll was in there, standing in a ring around someone or something that horrified the customers. I saw a mixture of fear and disgust on their faces as husbands and boy friends hustled their women to safety.

Joey broke through the ring and started shouting. By then, I'd gotten close enough to see what was causing the commotion.

There were two burly fellas. I recognized both of them. One had Joey's handiwork all over his face. It was the hood Joey had pistol-whipped in Claudette's bedroom, the sack of shit I hauled down to the curb. The second guy was Tweety's scar-faced pal, the one he'd been talking to on the street corner a few hours earlier.

That guy grinned at Joey and said, "The Big Four up in Cleveland wanted us to add a line to the letter they sent your dad."

Both thugs had their dicks out and were writing their postscript on the foyer's plush carpeting with a steady stream of pee.

Hunch grabbed the scar-faced guy by the balls and yanked him towards the coat check room, calling out to Joey and two of his security men, "C'mon, hold him."

The coat check gal shrieked as they pushed past her. She recoiled, trying to avoid being touched by the wet, floppy penis. She screamed and ran out from behind the counter.

A couple of the bouncers grabbed the other fella and held him in an arm lock. His arrogant grin quickly switched to a look of humiliation as he peed on his own shoes.

There was a lot of cursing coming out of the coat check room. I looked in time to witness Hunch, still holding the guy's balls, flick open a switchblade.

"Okay, Bruno, here's our answer," Hunch said.

Bruno? That name clicked with the face I'd thought was vaguely familiar.

Joey had Bruno's arms pinned behind his back. A quick flash of the blade cut through Bruno's belt. Then another removed the button holding his trousers together. A third sliced through the waistband of his white underwear.

With precise flicks of his wrist, Hunch proceeded to shave the black wiry hairs around Bruno's shriveled pecker. He was doing a nice, clean job of it. I looked back at the thug's face. Bruno. Beads of sweat were forming on his brow. Yep, it was Bruno Carpella. He didn't have that scar last time I saw him, and he'd grown into an ugly man.

Hunch finished his barbering job and shoved Bruno back out to the foyer, into the hands of several bouncers. "Now go home and show Red Masterson our answer."

The huddle of men pushed past me. Bruno stumbled over his dropped trousers and his eyes chanced to connect with mine. He did a slight double take and frowned. I knew, right then, he recognized me, too.

Bruno and his pal were tossed out the front door where a getaway car and driver were waiting. As they piled into the car, the driver gunned the engine. Kicking up a spray of gravel, they retreated into the night.

THE REST OF THE evening went by without a hitch. Nobody else tried to use The Oasis' foyer as a latrine.

By the time Joey'd gotten his staff to clean up the mess and we'd returned to the gaming room, Ginnie was back on stage for the second show. She must have gone straight home after the final jitterbug number because I didn't see her again.

At the end of the night, I sat in the upstairs office watching Joey and Hunch count the night's receipts. It was a lot of dough—guess the "dingdonging" incident didn't scare too many customers away. Still, Joey was fuming over it.

"Dammit," Joey said, as he rubber-banded a stack of twenties. "Those fuckers think they're gonna break us, like they did Pete Schmidt?"

Hunch was making piles of the silver collected from the slot machines. "That's how they started with Pete." He snorted. "But Red Masterson knows I'd cut off his dick if he tried that here."

Joey laughed. "So he sends Bruno and Manny."

I looked at Hunch and wondered why he didn't cut off Bruno's pecker right then and there. To my way of thinking, you better follow through on a threat, otherwise nobody takes you seriously. It's a dumb move to humiliate a guy like that—it only makes him want to hit back harder. Better to make him scared shitless of what you're capable of doing.

I didn't know how Hunch got to be head of security, but I was beginning to doubt it was on account of his brains.

J OEY WAS UNUSUALLY quiet as he drove us home to Fort Thomas. Halfway there, he blurted out, "*I* should've been the one to shave Bruno. Don't want those guys to think I'm gonna hide behind Hunch and let him do my family's fighting."

He lit up a cigarette and I left him to his thoughts.

We drove along in silence for a while.

It seemed like a good time to open up about recognizing Bruno. I hadn't said anything earlier because I didn't think it was anyone else's business.

"Joey, I know what a bastard Bruno is. I had some run-ins with him years ago."

That got Joey's attention. "You know him?"

"Yeah, from way back. Up until I left Cincinnati, when I was fifteen, Bruno and I sort of hung around together. We ran in the same pack and pretty much were fighting each other to be top dog. I'm not surprised what he's turned into."

"So you and him were just a couple of punks."

"Yeah. When I left, Bruno was still nursing the grudge he'd had against me for beating him up outside of Old Man Schuler's drugstore. I think we were only twelve when I did that. But he was a real bully—had it coming to him—always picked on smaller kids. The bastard zeroed in on a colored boy who'd walk down our block to get to his grandma's. Bruno didn't want 'those niggers moving in' he'd say. I stood up for the little kid, kept Bruno from beating him. Got called a nigger lover for that, so I figured I had to shut Bruno's mouth or he'd think he could walk all over me."

I was amazed to find myself getting mad all over again, just retelling the story. Funny how those old feelings stay with you.

Joey glanced at me as he pulled up the driveway. "Hard to imagine anyone thinking they could walk all over you."

I shrugged. "Did most of my growing afterwards, when I hit fourteen."

"You give him that scar?"

"Wish I had. No, someone else did the honors. Probably another guy who wouldn't take any of his crap."

"Did Bruno see you tonight?"

"Yep."

"Think he recognized you?"

"I know he did."

"Hmm. This is going to be interesting," Joey said.

We got out of the car and went around to the front door of his house. As he was putting his key in the lock, I said, "Oh, yeah, there's something else you might find interesting. Saw your hotshot saxophone player on the street in Newport talking to Bruno."

Joey was just about to push the door open. He turned and looked up at me. "Tweety? When was this?"

"Around seven. I was on my way to the club. Does that mean anything to you?"

"I don't know." Joey frowned. Then he said, more to himself than to me, "What would those two have to talk about?"

———

THWACK!
THWACK!
Bruno grunted with each swing of his hatchet.
Wood chips jumped high into the air.
Fucking guy thinks I'm just gonna let it drop?
THWACK!
This is just the beginning.
THWACK!
No way it ends like this.
THWACK!
Bruno left his hatchet stuck in the old tree stump and lumbered over to the heap of garbage piled up against a rickety shed.

This whole thing's fucked up. Good thing Manny and Al kept their mouths shut. First time I ever lied to Red. "Yeah, Red. Everything went okay. Me and Manny, we emptied all four kidneys."

He pulled out last year's Christmas tree and threw it over to the stump.

Shit, I'm screwed. He's bound to hear different from someone. And Red hates being lied to.

Bruno lifted the dead pine onto the stump.

I'm gonna end up like Dandy Charlie, sucking filthy, stinking river water into my lungs. And it'll be on account of that Oasis crowd—Hunch Williams, Joey Jules, and—and where the hell did Nick Cavanaugh suddenly come from? Fuck. I'll lay all their dicks out on this stump and—

Bruno tightened his claw-like fingers around the hatchet, raised it up over his head, and slashed down onto one of the dead tree's limbs.

THWACK!

The blade sliced clean through.

His loud laugh echoed off the brick building next door.

A light went on in his neighbor's third floor bedroom. A figure peered out the window.

Bruno looked up. The clouds in the night sky parted. The late summer moon suddenly illuminated the backyard, casting a spotlight down on him. Bruno bared his yellow fangs in a grin, making the jagged scar on his cheek pop out.

Bruno waved his hatchet and laughed again.

The neighbor ducked away from the window.

The light went off.

16

SEPTEMBER 20

"GOOD MORNING, MRS. JULES." One of Hunch's boys got up from his chair just outside Carl's hospital room. "This is the earliest I've seen you. It's only—" he looked at his watch. "What? Quarter after eight?"

Pearl said "good morning" back to him. "I'm turning into a day person," she added. "How's my husband doing?"

"Quiet night—I've been here since midnight. Sorry there's nothing new to report."

Pearl nodded. "Is someone coming soon to relieve you?"

"Yeah," he said, stifling a yawn, "should be here in about a half hour."

"Well, now that I'm here, you can go on home and get some sleep."

"Thank you, Mrs. Jules. See you tomorrow morning."

Pearl entered the room, praying she'd find Carl sitting up in bed. Or lying with his knees pulled up like he always did when he was just waking. But no such thing. Carl was on his back, arms and legs straight. The blankets around his body were perfectly smooth—not a ripple. He obviously hadn't wiggled a finger since the nurses had turned him and tucked him back in.

Pearl set her purse down on the bedside table, bent over her husband and kissed him on the forehead. She picked up a brush from the table and smoothed a couple of his unruly curls. She stroked his cheek, down his arm, and gently took hold of his hand as she lowered herself into her chair by the bed.

———

THE BLACK LIMOUSINE pulled right up to the front entrance of the hospital. Jimmy the Shiv, dressed in a dark blue pinstripe suit, emerged from the back and set his fedora on his head. He tugged on the French cuffs of his white shirt to make sure the gold cufflinks showed, and told the driver and the bodyguard riding shotgun in the front seat to stay put until he got back. This was the last leg of his tour of The Syndicate's business holdings in Ohio, and he wanted to cap it all off by gloating over Carl's immobile body.

Red Masterson had claimed over the phone, "It wasn't my boys who plugged him."

Jimmy didn't care who did it—he'd kiss whoever it was if it helped him get The Oasis. 'Course, now it meant he'd have to put the pressure on Pearl. Too bad, but business was business.

The woman at the front desk called out to him, as he walked past, "Oh, sir. *Sir!* It's not visiting hours yet."

"*Sono famiglia.* I'm family," Jimmy the Shiv said, over his shoulder, and kept right on walking until he got to the stairs. Red had given him Carl's room number, so he knew where he was going, and took his time climbing to the second floor.

The phone at the nurse's station began ringing as Jimmy pushed through the fire door and started down the corridor. On the way past the station, he touched the brim of his hat in a silent "good morning" to the old battle axe who'd picked up the phone.

———

PEARL KNEW SHE was going to have to go back to The Oasis. Carl wouldn't want her to spend the rest of her life sitting by his bed. In fact, she'd be more of a help to him if she did go back. Her presence at The Oasis would be an indication to everyone that the club would stay in the hands of the Jules family.

She'd show those bastards in Cleveland she was capable of running the whole show by herself and wasn't going to cave-in 'cause they were bigger and meaner and she was just a poor, helpless little old gal from the hills.

Pearl gave Carl's hand a squeeze, then heard someone entering the room. She looked towards the door.

GOD ALMIGHTY, SHE was still a gorgeous doll, Jimmy the Shiv thought as he stood in the doorway, staring at Pearl. This was an added pleasure—he wasn't sure he'd run into her. And now here he was, alone with her for the first time in over twenty years. And there was Carl, a vegetable. Talk about great timing. Play your cards right, Jimmy boy, and she'll see who's the *real* winner now.

"WHAT THE HELL you doing here, Jimmy, you dirty, stinking bastard," Pearl said, jumping to her feet.

The nurse came up behind Jimmy the Shiv, peered around him and said to Pearl, "I'm sorry, ma'am, he just walked right by."

Pearl put up her hand. "It's okay. Jimmy, come in and shut the door." As he obeyed and entered the room, she glanced towards her purse. Her chrome-plated .22 automatic was still nestled inside.

"I came to pay my respects to Carl," Jimmy said, "and offer my sympathies to you." He reached for Pearl's hand.

"Don't," she said, pulling away, "don't touch me, you lousy bullshitter." She took a little side step, closer to the table, and eyed her purse. "How dare you come here. Gonna finish the job yourself?"

Jimmy the Shiv held out his hands in an appeal. "Pearlie Mae." He crossed them over his heart. "Me?"

"Yeah, you. I read the letter your slimy lawyer sent us. You only show up in Newport when you're ready to come in for the kill. Last time was three years ago when you finally took over the Beverly Hills after putting Pete Schmidt through hell for four years."

"I had nothing to do with Carl's unfortunate situation. None of my associates in the area had nothin' to do with this. They assured me and I believe them. We were just starting negotiations. We're all friends. You and me and Carl, we go way back. We were just kids—remember?—knocking around that dirty little mining town. Now look at us. Successful. But *this?*" Jimmy said with a sweep of his arm towards Carl's motionless body. "This is too much for a little lady like you to handle by yourself."

"Fuck you."

"Pearlie Mae. Listen to me. I'm only thinking of you. Sign The Oasis over to The Syndicate and the Big Four will take care of you. They'll give you a percentage, let you oversee the place. You'll be able to give Carl all the medical attention he needs. The boys just want to help you, take care of you—"

"I don't want anyone taking care of me. I'm perfectly capable of taking care of myself. And Carl. We built The Oasis out of nothing and we have nothing to gain by handing it over to you guys."

"You're still a spitfire. Gutsy, too. Always loved that about you."

"Yeah? And you're still a dumb hood—always will be. You think you're a successful big shot? You're nothing but a puppet. Cleveland yanks your string and you jump. You haven't changed. Why do you think I dumped you for Carl? He's always been the better man. He had a dream, used his brains and went after it. Jimmy, the only way you got anything was by intimidating people and stealing from them."

Jimmy pointed at Carl. "You think I did this just to settle an old score that goes back to when we were kids?"

"You were always jealous of Carl and now you've come to steal *everything* he has."

"I just came here to pay my respects."

"Bull*shit*. You came to find out how close you were to taking his place in my bed."

Jimmy took a step forward. "God, Pearlie Mae—"

Pearl reached for her purse and slid it off the table.

Jimmy took another step. "Don't waste the rest of your life waiting for Rip van Winkle over there to wake up."

Pearl undid the clasp and reached in. "You come any closer and I'll—"

A sharp rap on the door stopped her. She looked at the door. So did Jimmy the Shiv.

The door slowly creaked open. A couple of men—one tall and wearing a cleric's collar, the second one shorter and wearing a yarmulke—poked their heads through the opening and peered into the room.

"May we come in?" asked the taller one.

"Oh. Father Zampella. Certainly." Pearl snapped her purse shut and held onto it. "Come in, come in. Hello, Rabbi Spandler."

The two visitors entered and exchanged "good mornings" with Pearl and Jimmy.

"Everybody in our congregation is praying for Carl," Father Zampella said.

Rabbi Spandler nodded. "Yes, yes. We're all praying. It's terrible what's happened to such a fine man."

"Thank you for coming," Pearl said. "I appreciate your prayers."

Father Zampella waved away her thanks. "It's the least we can do. You and your husband have been so generous—we could not have built our gym without your donations in the past."

"Yes, yes." Rabbi Spandler nodded. "And of course our library would not be what it is without your help. Ah, but now the bingo money goes into war bonds to stop that monster Hitler."

Pearl looked over the rabbi's head and caught a glimpse of Jimmy the Shiv's sarcastic smirk as he slowly backed out of the room.

Father Zampella and Rabbi Spandler moved to Carl's bedside and looked down on him. The priest put on his stole and crossed himself. "In nomine patris, et Filii, et Spiritus Sancti. Amen. Pater noster, qui es in coelis, santificétur nomen tuum . . . "

———

*P*EARLIE? PEARLIE? WHERE ARE YOU? Carl had to find her. He'd heard her shout the name "Jimmy"—someone was with her. She was shouting "dirty, stinking bastard," from somewhere down the long corridor.

He heard a man's voice. Jimmy Turelli's.

Carl stood in front of a door and listened. No. It was coming from further down the hall. He moved quickly to the next door.

Pearlie? It's me. I'm here. Nobody heard him. He still couldn't form the words.

Carl heard the voices again. Pearl and Jimmy the Shiv. Was she afraid? No. It wasn't fear. It was anger.

Pearlie. Carl tried to open a door. It was locked. He ran to the next one. It was locked, too. And the next and the next. *Where are you? I can't see you.*

"In nomine patris, et Filii, et Spiritus Sancti..." It was a third voice.

"Amen. Pater noster..."

Oh, God. No. She called a priest?

"...qui es in coelis..."

He tried to shout. *I'm not dying.*

"...santificétur nomen tuum..."

I'm not ready to die.

Carl ran down the corridor, throwing himself against every door, trying to break through.

Pearlie!

17

LOGBOOK ENTRY:

I WAS GETTING REALLY used to being chauffeured around town in a Cadillac. Joey and I drove through the bustling lunch hour traffic of Newport and parked outside an office building on Fourth and York, where we were supposed to meet Pearl. She had decided to make Joey a corporate officer in the family business. Guess the bills were piling up and, since Joey had turned twenty-one a few months ago and it was anyone's guess if Carl was ever going to sign anything again, it was logical that Joey be added as a signing officer.

We were early and amused ourselves watching the

secretaries go in and out of the building for maybe fifteen minutes before Pearl drove up in the DeSoto and parked in the spot behind us. She had spent the morning at Carl's bedside.

It had obviously been an upsetting morning. The first thing I noticed when she stepped out of the car was the hard set of her jaw, as if she was clenching her teeth. Her greeting was mechanical. She had a distracted look that said to me she was focused on inner thoughts more important than us.

When Joey asked what was new, she just shook her head. Whatever it was that preoccupied her, she wasn't going to share it at that moment.

A little guy, dressed in a red uniform and hat that made him look like an organ grinder's monkey, took us to the third floor in his stuffy elevator.

I sat in the lawyer's waiting room, twiddling my thumbs and thinking about what might be going through Pearl's head. The jerky *ratatatat* of the matronly secretary's stop-and-go method of typing kept invading my thoughts. She was a terrible typist. Seemed like every other word, she'd have to stop and flip through all her carbon copies to rub out some mistake. Each time, she'd peek over her typewriter and flash me a self-conscious smile.

I got tired of that, and found myself replaying the previous night's bizarre events in my head. I wasn't surprised at what Bruno had made of his life so far, but what the hell was the connection between him and Tweety?

———

"HOLD IT, HOLD IT," Doc Miller said, waving his hands. "You fellas can do better than that. Let's play that phrase again. Clean it up this time."

Annoyed, Raymond Twitty flipped back a page in his music and shook his head. *Jerks! We must've played "Chattanooga Choo Choo" a thousand times, and they still can't get it right.*

He brought the saxophone up to his lips, waited for Doc's downbeat, then played the bridge again.

"Okay, that was better. Raymond," Doc said, turning to him, "next time, give that B-flat more of a wail and hold it for three bars. Can you do it?"

Raymond cleared his throat and spoke from as deep down as he could. "Yeah, sure, Doc." His voice cracked on the "sure", and he got the usual ribbing. The clarinetist played three squeaky high C's and the rest of the band members added their chorus of "tweet, tweet, tweet."

Rage surged from Tweety's gut and pounded against the top of his head, threatening to blow out his temples. His fists tightened around the keys of his saxophone. *Assholes, they're assholes, nothing but assholes.*

Doc tapped a pencil on the edge of his metal music stand. "Okay, kiddies, recess time is over. Let's get back to work. Now, Tweety—ah—*Raymond*, remember the wail."

Raymond fumed through the rest of *Chattanooga Choo Choo, Brazil,* and especially *The Woodpecker Song*— when the clarinetist played the high notes of Woody Woodpecker's laugh with squeaky *tweets*. Every time he did that, the rest of the band members howled with laughter, making a shambles of the rehearsal.

Finally, Raymond shot out of his seat and turned to the clarinetist. "Stop wasting our time, damn it! Do that once more and I'll shove that licorice stick down your throat."

"All of you shut the fuck up!" Doc yelled. "And Raymond, sit down."

"Well, I can see things haven't changed since I've been away." The woman's voice echoed across the empty Caravan Room.

Raymond turned, along with everyone else on the bandstand, towards the entrance. *My God, it's Pearl. How long has she been standing there?* He sat back down in his seat and watched her walk across the room towards the band, smiling, radiant like an angel. Her son Joey and that big pal of his, Nick, trailed in behind her.

Oh, brother, have I screwed it all up? I'm supposed to be the stable, intelligent one around here. She knows that. That's what she likes about me. I was only trying to get them to stop acting like a bunch of schoolyard kids. She must've seen that. She's smiling at everyone but me. Shit, now she thinks I'm just like the rest of these goons. She's saying something to Doc—my head hurts, I can't hear right. Oh, Pearl, Pearl, don't be disappointed in me. She's looking at the band and talking. What is she saying?

Raymond took a deep breath. His head cleared.

"You're all family to me," Pearl said, scanning the faces of the band members, "and I need and appreciate your support in this terrible situation. I want you to know that any rumors about my selling The Oasis are false—nothing but a pack of lies probably started by those Cleveland bums. I'll never sell out to them. Or to anyone else for that matter. You're sounding great, boys."

Pearl looked directly at Raymond, and winked. *Ha! Did the others see that? No. It's still our secret.* Raymond smiled back at Pearl. *Yes. Yes. I will always support you.* He shot a quick look at his tormentors and sneered. *You bastards'll be jealous. Pearl and me. She might turn to you for support, but she'll come to me for comfort.*

———

LOGBOOK ENTRY:

I WAS STILL PUZZLING over the Bruno-Tweety connection as we walked into the Caravan Room. At that very moment, Tweety jumped out of his seat and threatened the clarinetist. The sax player's face was beet red, and I was almost convinced his pipe cleaner arms really did have the strength to shove that licorice stick down the guy's throat.

Tweety's little temper tantrum hadn't upset Pearl at all. She gave the band a little pep talk, reassuring them the club would stay in Jules hands and thanked them for their support.

We sat at one of the front tables and watched the rehearsal. It was obvious Pearl was in her element. She looked relaxed and happy, even when Joey went Navy and whistled at the chorus girls when they came out and did some hot Mexican number. But her face tightened up again as she leaned close to Joey and said, "Jimmy Turelli's in town."

"Jimmy the Shiv?" Joey said, his eyes getting that slightly crazed look in them.

Pearl stabbed at the table top with a long, red fingernail. "Don't be stupid and go looking for trouble."

It was a private conversation, so I kept my eyes on

Tweety, who had his eyes on us.

Joey asked Pearl how she knew this Jimmy the Shiv was in town.

"Never mind how I know—I'm just telling you this in case he shows up here. I don't want *you* starting anything," she said, putting an end to that topic.

There was something strange about Tweety. I realized he wasn't looking at us. He was looking at Pearl. Every once in a while, his eyes would flick down to his music, but pop right back up and lock on her.

Pearl had switched to the more mundane business of the bills piling up on her desk. She and Joey talked about meat rationing and who they'd have to go to on the black market to make up the difference, while on stage the girls strutted back and forth, twirling their skirts and showing off a lot of leg.

Tweety kept his eyes on Pearl. It wasn't just a casual look, it was intense. And it became apparent to me that Tweety and I had something in common. I hoped I'd done a better job of hiding my feelings about Pearl than he was at that moment.

———

GINNIE FINISHED tightening the ankle straps on her high-heeled shoes, and stuck a couple of hat pins into her sombrero to keep it from flying off during the rehearsal of the *Down Mexico Way* number. She joined the other dancers in their bright yellow and red costumes as they all filed out the dressing room and headed towards the stage in the Caravan Room.

"Ouch!" She felt the strap of her little halter top snap against her bare back. "Hey!" She wheeled around and glared at Sally.

Sally glared back. "You better know this routine, honey. I gotta dance with a sore ankle thanks to you and your drunken stumbling last night."

"I just lost my balance. I wasn't drunk."

"You were so—could smell it on your breath. All the other gals noticed too, but they're all too polite to say anything."

"I lost count for a second and took an extra step. Nobody's perfect. Not even *you*. Cripes!"

"Cut the chatter," the dancer in front of Ginnie whispered over her shoulder, just before she stepped out onto the stage.

Ginnie pasted on her smile and grabbed her skirts. Flaring them out, she took her place in the chorus line as hip-swinging, Mexican beauty number five.

Someone greeted the dancers with a loud wolf whistle.

Ginnie looked out at the tables. Pearl, Nick, and Joey were sitting front and center. Joey was doing all the whistling, but he didn't seem to be aiming it at any one particular dancer.

Ginnie hiked up her skirts so the front slit in her costume showed off more of her tight satin panties.

As the trumpets blared and her turn to promenade across the front of the stage came up, she straightened her shoulders, pushing her breasts out as far as they'd go and added a sultry swing to her hips. At that moment, Joey turned to say something to his mother, and they got into some important conversation that lasted through the rest of the routine. Ginnie never did catch Joey's eye. Even Nick wasn't watching her and seemed to have his attention focused on the band the entire time.

Ginnie flounced off the stage at the end of the

176

rehearsal, frustrated to the point of tears. How could Joey do this to her? It was almost as though she'd been invisible. She couldn't go back into that dressing room until she'd had a chance to talk to him, to be near him.

Ginnie broke off from the rest of the dancers filing into the dressing room and exited through the side door, so she could make her way back to the main entrance of the Caravan Room and catch Joey on the way out.

By the time Ginnie got there, Joey and Pearl had already left the room and were heading towards the stairs to go up to the offices.

"Joey," she called out.

Both mother and son stopped, and looked in her direction. Pearl frowned at her.

Ignoring her look, Ginnie said, "I need to talk to you, Joey."

"I'll be up in a few minutes," he said to his mother.

Pearl's frown didn't leave her face. Without a word, she turned and climbed the stairs to her office.

"Okay, Ginnie. What's up?"

"Come in here with me." Ginnie clutched at the lapel of Joey's jacket and pulled him into the dealers' break room. She slammed the door behind her, and clicked the lock. Throwing her arms around his neck, she pressed her lips against his.

Joey didn't respond to the kiss. "Ginnie, this isn't the time to—"

She took his hand and slid it under her halter top, guiding it to her nipple. "I think it's a perfect time."

Joey started to pull his hand out, but Ginnie held it tight and put it back where she wanted it.

"Hmm, Ginnie. You're suddenly very adventurous."

"Maybe it's this costume. You didn't watch the number. I was dancing for you." She reached behind her back, unhooked her top and pulled it off. "Maybe I was just wearing too much. Is this better?" Ginnie said, pressing up against him.

Joey reached under her skirt and peeled off her red satin panties.

18

JIMMY THE SHIV'S MORNING hadn't gone the way he wanted it to. Sure, he'd gotten a chance to gloat over Carl's comatose body, and yeah, he did get the added surprise of seeing Pearl again. But she didn't exactly greet him with open arms.

Carl's coma raised new problems. What if he stayed that way? Could Pearl sign over The Oasis by herself? What would happen if Carl died? Jimmy needed to know from Charles Lester if Carl's condition presented an opportunity or had thrown up a roadblock. Who the hell knew what the laws were in Kentucky?

Jimmy was pissed off at not finding Lester in his office. When he'd asked the receptionist where the lawyer was, she'd said, "I don't know, sir. He just said he had some people to meet and papers to file, and would be gone all day."

Dammit. What good was having Lester on a retainer if the son of a bitch wasn't going to be around when you needed him? "You find your boss and tell him Jimmy Turelli's waiting to talk to him at the Merchants Club."

———

"WHAT ARE YOU GAWKING AT?" Bruno shouted at Al.

Al shrugged innocently. "I'm just trying to imagine what it feels like."

"Like I got sandpaper shorts on. What the fuck d'ya think it feels like?" Bruno spun around to Manny. "I don't wanna hear another word about it from either one of you. And if I catch you staring at my crotch, I'll dig out your eyeballs and serve 'em back to you in a martini."

"All right, *all right!* We get it," Al said, throwing his hands up in front of him.

Bruno sat on his bar stool in the Yorkshire Club, staring into his liquid lunch. Bad enough the whole damn story about what happened at The Oasis was already on the streets, elaborated with lies about his balls being cut off. But he'd lied to Red and now Red had called him up that morning, wanting to talk to him. Bruno looked at his watch. Ten more minutes before he had to be at the Merchants Club.

This was it—the end of Bruno Carpella. He downed his drink.

"What do you want us to do?" Al asked.

"Go fuck yourself." Bruno walked out the door and down York to Fourth Street, oblivious to all the street traffic. All Bruno could think was that the truth had reached Red's ears. What was Red going to do to him?

Bruno was a few yards from the Merchants Club when he saw three guys in suits walking ahead of him. He recognized the one in the dark blue pinstripe and fedora. "Oh, shit. Jimmy the Shiv. That's all I need," he said, under his breath. "How the hell did he find out I screwed up and get down here from Cleveland so fast?"

Bruno slowed his step and watched the three men enter the Merchants Club. He wanted to stay outside, smoke a cigarette and think about what to say, but he couldn't be late for his meeting with Red.

Bruno stopped at the front door. He pulled a handkerchief out of his pocket, lifted his hat and wiped the sweat off his brow. The hat went back on his head at a rakish tilt. He straightened his tie, took a deep breath, then pushed open the front door.

The dining room was packed. Bruno spotted Red at his usual table in an isolated corner. Jimmy the Shiv was just taking a seat across from him. The other two guys were at the bar. Bruno started to wind his way around the tables.

Most of the lunch time crowd were clerks and officials from the courthouse down the street. This wasn't high class like the Yorkshire Club, but it was Red's territory—and Bruno suddenly felt like he had to take a crap. He needed to mop his brow again. Sweat trickled from his armpits. He couldn't barge in on the conversation Jimmy the Shiv was having with Red, so he just stood, at a respectful distance, waiting.

Jimmy's back was to him, but Bruno had a full view of Red's face. Damn, he wished he could read lips.

Red saw Bruno and summoned him with a flick of his finger. Oh God, was he going to have to explain what happened last night to Jimmy?

"Jimmy Turelli," Red said. "Bruno Carpella."

Jimmy nodded.

"Bruno here's in charge of bothering the Jules into signing the papers," Red explained. He indicated the chair next to him with a jerk of his head. "Sit down, Bruno. I know I asked you to meet me here for lunch, but that was before I knew Jimmy was going to honor us with a visit."

Bruno obeyed and kept his mouth shut.

Jimmy glanced at Bruno, made a little grunting noise, then turned back to Red. "So, no one knows where the hell Lester is, huh? Well, I can't sit here all day, waiting for him."

"His secretary doesn't know?" Red asked.

Jimmy shook his head.

"Since when? She *always* knows where he is and what he's doing. She can tell you when he last took a leak."

"Yeah, well, I don't like it." Jimmy turned to Bruno. "So, what've you been doing to bother the Jules?"

Here it comes, Bruno thought. He cleared his throat. "We dingdonged The Oasis last night."

Jimmy's laugh sent spit flying across the table. "Just like you did to Pete Schmidt, huh, Red?"

Red shrugged. "Yeah. Start scaring the customers away. It's a beginning. And even if the Jules don't take it seriously, we just keep going back and find new ways to bother them until they do. *Right*, Carpella?"

Bruno saw in his boss's look that he was getting off

this time but he'd better not screw up again.

Red ordered lunch for them. Bruno picked at his pork chop and kept quiet, while Jimmy and Red discussed going after Buck Brady and his Primrose Club. By the time their apple pie was served, they were on to the Negro numbers racket and White Smitty, "that pale-skinned jigaboo," who had a big share of the action.

Jimmy squirmed in his seat and looked around the room. It was half-empty—the lunch time crowd was moving out. "Nice food, nice place, but I can't stay here the rest of my life. Where the hell's that Lester? I can't go back to Cleveland without seeing him."

Red said, "You don't need to be stuck here. I'll wait for Lester." He turned to Bruno. "Take Jimmy over to Sophie's."

"Huh?" Bruno was not ready for this.

"You heard me."

"She ain't open yet." Bruno wasn't about to confess he was on her shit-list—one more screw-up was sure to put him on Red's.

Red frowned. "Tell her it's a favor to me." He leaned over to Jimmy. "I'll know where to get you when Lester shows up. Ask for Claudette."

BRUNO SAT WITH JIMMY in the back seat of the limousine, and directed the driver to Sophie's.

Here I am, Bruno thought, sitting with one of the big shots. He'd dreamed of this situation so many times, he'd lost count. This had been one of his goals, but instead of enjoying it, he was doing everything he could to keep from puking all over Jimmy's snazzy suit. He didn't know how Sophie was going to react when she saw him. You don't slam the door in the face of someone like Jimmy the Shiv. It would all be his fault. No forgiveness from Red this time. As soon as she opened that door, he'd tell her who he had with him. That'll impress her—put him back in her good book.

Bruno jumped out of the limousine as it was rolling to a halt outside Sophie's.

"You're kinda jumpy," Jimmy said, as he got out. "Is there a problem?"

"No, no. Sorry."

The bodyguard got out of the front seat and brought up the rear as Bruno led Jimmy up the steps to the front door. Bruno wiped his damp palm on his pant leg and pushed the buzzer.

A few seconds later, Sophie swung the door open. "What d'ya want?" Her look of disgust changed to one of interest as she took in the sight of the well-dressed man standing next to Bruno.

"Sophie," Bruno said, quickly, "this is Jimmy Turelli from Cleveland."

"Oh," she said, her face brightening, "I would never have recognized you. Those newspaper photos don't do you justice. You've come to see one of my girls?"

Bruno stepped aside to let Jimmy go in first. "Red said—"

"Welcome, Mr. Turelli." Sophie waved him in.

The bodyguard pushed past Bruno and followed Jimmy the Shiv.

This is gonna work out okay, Bruno thought, as he took a step to go in. He caught a glimpse of Sophie's scowl just before she slammed the door in his face.

"Sophie?"

The lock clicked into place.

———

P EARL SWISHED THE ice chips around in her Coca-Cola with a straw and reread the letter from Charles Lester. She studied the creases in the paper and imagined Carl scrunching it up in anger. If only she hadn't been sick that night and been here at the club as usual, maybe things would have gone differently.

Pearl looked at Hunch, who'd joined her at the bar. "It's not an easy decision to make," she said. "I hate leaving Carl lying in that hospital bed by himself. But I've got to start spending time here at the club. Carl would want me to do that."

"How much longer is Joey going to be here?" Hunch asked.

"A few more days and he's flying back to San Diego. You and Doc have been lifesavers, but with this Lester thing going on," Pearl shook the lawyer's letter, "I've gotta show everyone I'm taking charge. I'm gonna spend the first part of my afternoons at the hospital, and the rest of my time here. I'll be in every day."

Hunch leaned a little closer towards her. "I can speak for the staff—everyone's with you. But you should know that some of the dealers have been approached by Schmidt and Brady and even Sleepout Louie. Those guys are trying to put a bug in their ears about this place folding up. That you're bound to sell out and their jobs ain't too secure."

"I've heard the gossip. Nobody expects me to succeed. But I've been just as much a part of running The Oasis as Carl. Eight years I've been here almost every day. I know this business as well as any of those other club owners out there. I'll show them."

"Yes, you will."

"I have one fear though, Hunch. And I'll only say it once. To you." Pearl looked him in the eye. "What if Carl never comes out of this and spends the rest of his life a vegetable? Lying there in bed? I don't know how I'd handle that."

Pearl felt the tears coming and reached into her purse for a handkerchief. Hunch looked away as she dabbed at her eyes and blew her nose. She reached into her purse again and rummaged around in the bottom, under her gun. "Where's my lipstick?"

She got up from the stool, went behind the bar, and opened a drawer under the cash register. "Got one in here somewhere," Pearl said, pushing aside pencils and pads and loose rubber bands. "Well, *that's* strange. Where is it?"

———

RAYMOND TWITTY WALKED INTO the men's room, went into one of the stalls and locked the door. He took the small gold tube out of his pocket. For a moment, he held it in his hand and squeezed it. Raymond's eyes closed as a feeling of warmth flooded his body.

He slid the top off the lipstick case, held it up to his nose and breathed in.

"Oh, Pearl."

He pictured her leaning across the counter behind the bar and looking between the liquor bottles into the mirror, the fabric of her evening gown straining, holding in her breasts. He'd watched her paint her beautiful lips with this tube of lipstick, night after night.

What color did she like? Raymond looked at the label. "Military red. I like that, too."

Slowly, he twisted the base of the tube until a half inch of the creamy red stick was visible. The sight of it sent another rush of tingling heat up his legs.

It had touched Pearl's lips.

He kissed it.

Another rush of pleasure.

They were finally touching.

Raymond slowly pushed the lipstick around, smearing the taste of her on his own lips.

19

HE LOOKS SO MUCH like my Carmelo, Pearl thought as she straightened the loops of Joey's bow tie. So handsome. So strong. But this moodiness, this anger... She studied her son's face—the hard glint in his eyes, the downturn of his lips, the way he held his jaw. He got that from her.

They'd come home together in the Cadillac, having given Nick the DeSoto to go out on the town on his own. Pearl had expected it to be a perfect opportunity to talk with Joey alone, but all the way home he'd kept his eyes on the road and conversed—if you could call it that—with nothing more than grunts and head nods. He seemed so far away, lost in an angry world.

Pearl worried about him. Soon, they'd have to return to the club. Here in his bedroom would be her only chance for the rest of the evening to talk to him alone.

She finished straightening Joey's tie, then stroked his cheek. "I hate to let you go. This visit has gone too quickly."

"I should stay, Mom. You can't go through this by yourself."

Pearl gave his cheek a playful slap. "Of course I can. You're talking to your mother, not some little old lady."

"No, I'm serious. I should stay."

"You crazy? Think, Joey. You gotta go back. You go AWOL and the Navy'll throw you in the brig for a couple of years and what the hell good'll you do me in there? Until this war's over, that's what you gotta do."

"Yeah, well, I don't see how I'm doing you *or* my country any good breaking up fights and hauling in drunks."

"Just go back and do your duty."

"My duty is to make sure Jimmy the Shiv knows that he and Cleveland are going to have to fight me, too."

Pearl placed her hands on Joey's chest. "I told you, don't get involved in this." She could feel the shoulder holster under his jacket. No use telling him not to carry his gun—that would be stupid. After all, she had hers.

"Right now, Jimmy's probably thinking I'm just your little boy. What if Dad doesn't make it? I become head of the family."

"Oh? Why's that? Just because you're a man? I can handle this."

"Mom, Cleveland won't take a dame seriously."

189

"I'll show them they'd better."

"That'll make it even worse. You'll have everybody in town thinking I'm just your little boy, hiding behind your skirts."

"Joey, I've gotta make them understand they have to deal with me here and now. Besides, your father will make it—he's not dead."

"Ma, be realistic."

"What? You giving him up for dead? How could you?"

"Shit, Ma."

"Don't you 'shit, Ma' *me*."

Joey flung his hands up in the air and turned away from her. "No sense talking to you." He stomped out of the room.

Pearl felt sick, her stomach twisted into knots. *God.* She sank down onto the edge of Joey's bed and held her head in her hands.

Why is this happening? she thought. *I can't talk to my son anymore. All I wanted was to tell him to be careful and keep his head on straight. I just wanted him to know that I loved him and didn't want anything to happen to him. How could I have let this get out of hand? Oh Carl, you've got to come back.*

———

*A*LL THESE DOORS. It seemed like Pearl was behind every one of them.

Carl felt his lungs working hard to breathe.

In, then out. In, then out.

His legs felt heavy, like they were encased in

190

concrete. He dragged himself up and down the corridor.

Pearl? Pearlie Mae? She needed him—he was certain of it.

But he didn't have the energy anymore to push against the locked doors.

——

"HEY, BRUNO, what's with the rough stuff?" Al asked. "That old guy's always made good."

"I don't care. He was late with this payment and that's that." Bruno shoved the fifty bucks into his pocket and crossed the old man's name off the list in his note pad. He pushed the spiral edge of the pad up against Al's nose, squashing his nostrils until they looked like a porker's snout. "You're in no position to criticize."

Bruno, Manny, and Al were standing outside the Stork Club on Monmouth Street. It was only 8:00 P.M., but Bruno had been on a rampage since getting locked out of Sophie's that afternoon. He was making the rounds, hitting everyone whose name appeared in his little book.

Bruno checked the list. "Some of these jokers'll be over at the 345 Club by now." He looked up in time to see Red Masterson's maroon convertible pass by on his nightly rounds. Not even a wave. Ah, that's okay, Bruno thought, Red probably didn't see me.

But a couple of stooges who worked for Sleepout Louie did. "Hey, Carpella," one of them shouted from across the street. "I hear they've got your balls bronzed and hanging over the bar at The Oasis."

Shit. How fuckin' humiliating. What was he supposed to do now? Wear a sign around his neck saying "They were only shaved"?

———

LOGBOOK ENTRY:

I ONLY HAD another twenty-four hours before I had to catch the train to start my three-day trip back to San Diego. The days had gone by too fast. I'd only just started to scratch the surface of Little Mexico—there were so many stories here. I just wanted to see as much as I could of the place before leaving.

Driving the DeSoto, I left The Oasis around 5:00 P.M. and breathed in the faint scent of Pearl's perfume all the way to downtown Newport. Joey was only interested in pointing me to the swankier spots in town, but when I told him I wanted to see one or two of the bustout joints, he made a face, then shrugged his shoulders and gave me a few names of places to take a look at.

I spent some time at Esselman's Cafe and the Old Dogpatch. Pretty dreary places with not many customers, but maybe it was too early in the evening. Found myself driving past the police station on Fourth Street and remembered Joey saying something about a 345 Club nearby on Central. Shouldn't be too hard to find, I thought, turning the corner. Some of the club names were just their street addresses.

Sure enough, right between Fourth and Third was the club at 345 Central.

Inside, I was greeted by the bartender's, "Girls and games upstairs." I could hear laughter coming from the second floor.

"Can I get a beer down here?" I said, settling onto a stool at the bar.

The owner of this place didn't go in for fancy decor, either—it was just as dark and dreary as the other two clubs. Everything in the bar looked old, beaten up, and covered with a layer of dust. Guess nothing much happened down on this level. One look at the bartender's dirty fingernails as he set a greasy glass in front of me made me decide to drink from the beer bottle instead.

I took a couple of swigs, then tried to get the bartender into a conversation. Maybe pry some stories out of him. No dice. The guy was the exact opposite of Gabby over at the Joseph Hotel. He had a weariness about him that said he'd probably seen too much.

A couple of times, the door opened and men in groups of twos and threes would enter the club and head straight for the stairs without any need for direction from the bartender.

I was just finishing my beer and thinking about climbing the stairs to see the sights myself, when another group of customers came in and sat down at the bar, two stools from me. I looked up and was about to give them a friendly greeting. Then I realized it was Bruno Carpella and his two pals.

Bruno showed me his yellow teeth. "Well, well," he said, "if it ain't the nigger lover, himself. Where you been all these years?"

Oh, God. Here comes trouble. I shrugged my shoulders and said, "Here. There. All over. Mostly at sea. I'm here on leave."

"So you joined up, huh. Duty called." Bruno turned and ordered a shot of bourbon. The other two just sat there and waited in silence.

I asked, "What about you?"

Bruno watched the bartender pour his drink. "4-F."

I waited for him to elaborate on the reason for his physical deferment, but he kept his mouth shut. Looking him up and down, there weren't any obvious deformities, and I'd already seen at The Oasis that he had the right number of body parts down below. I figured it was something like flat feet. Or maybe it was his hands. Bruno's hands had always looked weird. Part-animal, part-human. Large mitts with short, thin digits that looked more like claws than usable fingers.

I studied the scar on his face. Ha, the guy was probably rejected 'cause he was just too damn ugly.

Bruno studied *me* with hooded eyes. "Since when are you on the Jules' payroll?"

"I'm not on their payroll. Told you, I'm on leave. Just visiting."

"Oh, yeah? If you're just visiting, how come you're spending so much time on this side of the river? Why you helping those assholes over at The Oasis, instead of helping your old man with his chili parlor?"

I ignored the bit about my old man. "Joey Jules is a shipmate of mine. We're stationed at San Diego and we're both here on leave."

Bruno turned to one of his goons. "Hey, Al. This is the fella who beat you up at Sophie's, right?"

I said, "Wait a minute—"

"Yeah, that's him," Al said. "Right, Manny?"

The other sack of shit, Manny, said, "Yeah, him and that Joey Jules were the ones who roughed us up."

Bruno threw back his drink, slammed the glass down

on the bar, and said, "Cavanaugh, you always chose the wrong side. See ya 'round."

As if on cue, the three stooges got off their bar stools and left. Bruno didn't pay for his bourbon. The bartender didn't seem to care. "Hey pal," he said to me, "you want another beer?"

"Yeah, sure."

I heard the door open and felt someone pass behind me, heading for the stairs. I turned to watch the guy go up.

A coldness gripped my stomach.

I was no longer twenty-three years old—I was a gawky teenager. And that was my old man.

I think. I only caught a glimpse of his back, and he was a good fifteen feet away. But the guy moved like him. I was sure it was him.

"Never mind the beer," I said and watched Mister Perfect disappear in search of the sleazy delights upstairs.

"You all right, pal?" The bartender eyed me. "Want something else?"

"No. No. I'm just gonna sit here for a minute. Do you know that guy who just came in?"

"Not personally. But he's a regular. Comes in once a week."

I stared at the bartender for a few seconds. "You know his name?"

"Nope." He went back to wiping the greasy glasses.

So, what was Mister Nobody-can-do-anything-as-good-as-me doing in a dive like this? What kind of lies did he hand my mother to cover up where he was going?

Nothing I did was ever good enough for that old man. Never could please him. "You got a C+ in school?" he'd say,

"Hell, Nicholas, you can do better than that? B+? Hell, it's about time. Quitting school? You come and work in the chili parlor. Pull your weight, earn your keep in this family. You're putting too much meat in the pot. No, no, no. That's too little. How many times do I gotta tell you? Chop the cheese *this* way, not *that* way. Where did you learn to mop a floor? It wasn't from me or your mother."

And the way he stirred his coffee. He'd count while he stirred twenty times. Not eighteen or nineteen or twenty-one. It had to be exactly twenty. Then he'd tap his spoon twice on the side of the cup. Drove me nuts.

"No, no, *no*, Nicholas. Stack the cans of beans on *this* shelf, not *that* one. A place for everything and everything in its place. Stop day dreaming, boy. You don't have the sense God gave a flea."

He finally got so tired of me, he stopped talking to me—just took the jobs outta my hands and did everything himself. Didn't talk to me for months. Fuck him. I left. In the middle of the night.

I didn't like leaving mom, but I was afraid I'd kill that man of hers if I stayed under their roof. Wrote to her a few times, but I never got anything back. How could I? Kept moving around so much, nothing ever caught up with me. After a couple of years, I just quit trying. But I swore I'd never go back to that greasy spoon chili parlor of his until I was a big shot with enough cash in my hip pocket to buy that old bastard's place several times over.

I wondered about my kid brother Jim. How old was he when I left? Four? Five? He'd be what? Thirteen, now? Was he cleaning pots and pans in the old man's kitchen? Wiping down tables? Or was he planning to escape like me?

Eight years I'd been away from my old man, traveling around the world, and now our paths were crossing in a dingy bar. I wasn't sure I wanted to confront him at that moment, but something was pushing me to go up those stairs. Guess I just needed to get a good look at him doing something Mister Perfect shouldn't be doing. Hell, this was a *good* time to confront him.

I paid for my beer and climbed the stairs.

The action was taking place in a large room that still was pretty drab, except for the young busty gals prancing around in slinky slips and shorts. There must have been thirty guys up there, some trying their luck at the row of slot machines along the near wall, others crowding around a blackjack table in the center of the room.

I spied Mister Perfect staring at his hand of cards, while a gal half his age hung onto his arm. But I was still just getting the back view. His haircut was the same as I remembered—close on the sides and slicked back on top.

Keeping my distance, I walked around the perimeter of the room to get a look at his face. As his profile came into view, I started thinking I'd made a mistake. He was the same body type as my old man, maybe heavier, but he was smiling. Didn't remember seeing much of that.

I caught sight of his full face.

I stared.

It wasn't him.

I was pissed.

Got myself so worked up, I'd *wanted* to confront him. Right there.

Hell. Now what?

Take a trip across the river?

Sure, why not?

Got a car. Got an expensive suit on and some money in my pocket.

I didn't look like a failure.

Some fresh-faced gal sidled up to me, making sure I had a good look down the crevice between her breasts. "Well, hello—"

"Sorry," I said, removing her hand from my arm. "Nothing personal, but I gotta be someplace else."

She gave me a wide-eyed look. "*This* is a good place to be."

"Looking for someone," I said, and hurried across the room and down the stairs.

It must have been Bruno's comment about my father and his chili parlor that brought all that stuff to the surface and had me ready to see my old man around every corner.

Best to get this over with right now.

I pushed out the door of the 345 Club. The sun had finally set. The streets were dark. I started down the sidewalk towards where I'd parked the car.

"What's your hurry?" The question came from my right.

Turning, I found myself looking down an alleyway.

Bruno's face appeared out of the darkness. The rest of him followed. He lunged towards me, his claws going right for my eyes.

I grabbed his lead arm and, in one movement, pulled, turned sideways, and lashed out my right foot, kicking both his legs out from underneath him. Then I let go of his arm and sent him flying into the gutter.

Footsteps came up behind me. I quickly spun around. Manny was right in my face. I ducked his round house swing, and came up with a left to his chin. I followed with a right-left combination, connecting with the sore spots left over from Joey's pistol-whipping. Manny went down real fast—a classic glass jaw. Al, right behind him, swung a blackjack at my head. I blocked with my left and countered with my right, staggering him.

Where was Bruno? *Watch your back.*

I snapped my head from side to side, trying to get Bruno in my sights. He was fast—two steps out of the gutter and he slammed his shoulder into my gut, knocking the wind out of me. I blindly reached out, grabbing him around his neck as we both fell to the ground. I tried to twist his neck as we rolled around on the sidewalk, but lost my grip. Bad position. Had to get to my feet. I kicked him away and righted myself.

On my left, Manny had glued his jaw back together and was coming back for more. Al swung in from my right with his blackjack. Bruno was behind me. The three of them charged. Me, I was the bullseye—no place to run to. I fisted my hands and swung my arms with as much force as I could. Bruno's claws grabbed my neck from behind and dug in. Al's blackjack crashed on my skull and a flashing pattern of stars exploded in front of my eyes. Manny grabbed my right arm and twisted, bringing it up behind my back. Gritting my teeth, I tried to punch his face with my left fist. Al blocked it. Catching my wrist in the crook of his elbow, he wrapped his other arm around mine. They had me, and they knew it.

Bruno smiled as he watched them drag me into the alley. "Okay, nigger lover. We've got a score to settle with you

Oasis boys. We're gonna send your pal Joey and his mom a message. And you're gonna be the messenger." He laughed.

"What're you gonna do?" I asked, "Piss on me?"

Bruno's laugh snapped into a snarl and he slammed my jaw with his fisted paw.

I struggled against his goons—even managed to land a kick to Bruno's balls—but Manny and Al had me tight. Bruno got his wind back, and started slugging my face with lefts and rights.

———

THIS IS BETTER THAN SEX, Bruno thought as he smashed his fist into Cavanaugh's mug. All the humiliation heaped on him the last few days powered his punches. Being locked out of Sophie's. Getting his crotch shaved.

He'd show them he wasn't someone to be laughed at. Bruno landed a solid right in the pit of Cavanaugh's stomach.

God, I could kill him right now. Bruno smiled to himself. *It would be so easy. Then what? Naw, rough up pretty boy just enough to make 'em scared of what we'll do next. They'll get the message.*

Bruno stopped swinging, and stepped back to admire the damage. Nick's head rolled from the force of his last punch, then slumped onto his chest.

"Look at the sailor boy," Bruno said to Manny and Al, who were keeping Nick up on his feet. "He ain't so tough."

"So, what d'ya want to do with him?" Al asked.

"Leave him here in the alley," Bruno said, rubbing his raw knuckles.

Manny and Al let go of Nick's arms. Nick sank to the ground.

Bruno said, "Okay, let's blow."

"Yeah," Al said, looking up and down the street, "we gotta get outta here before some cop drives by."

"Oooh, I'm scared." Bruno wiggled his fingers in the air. He spat, aiming the clam at a spot two inches from Cavanaugh's nose, then eyed his two stooges with disgust. "Manny, cover fuckin' Nervous Nellie here while she makes a run for the car."

Bruno shoved his paws into his pocket and sauntered out of the alley.

20

POPE AND DUCKER HAD TAKEN time out from pounding the pavement to grab a coffee at Benny's Diner.

"Okay," Pope said, "we must've been to all the day and night houses on Second Street—"

"And if you'd listened to me," Ducker snapped, "we'd have skipped all that! Just 'cause some bartender we questioned at The Oasis said Carl Jules still likes to play patty-cake with the gals down on the 'Bottoms', don't make it so. The guy sure likes his women, I won't argue that. But I'm telling you, Carl Jules ain't the type to go down there. He only goes for the cream."

"Yeah, well," Pope said, ignoring his cousin's

grouchiness, "we've been to almost every whorehouse in town. If you believe what they all say, Carl wasn't cheating on his wife with a prostitute."

Ducker blew on his cup of coffee. "More likely he'd be doing that than fooling around with one of his dancers. Think he learned his lesson after getting that poor little girl pregnant a few years back."

"Well," Pope said, "we still haven't been to Vivian's, Sophie's, or Cooky's."

Ducker banged his cup down on the counter and rubbed his eyes. "This is a fuckin' waste of time. No madam is gonna tell us who their johns are—*especially* Sophie."

"So, what do you wanna do? Call Mrs. Jules in again for questioning and ask, 'Oh, could you please bring in all your guns so we can check them, because we think you might have been pissed off at your husband and shot him?'"

"Ha. Ha. Ha."

An uneasy silence settled in between the two detectives.

Pope looked away from his partner, took a deep breath and let it go. "So Joey Jules was right? We're just gonna sit on our fat asses and do nothing?"

Ducker stared out the window.

Pope got up off his stool and tossed a nickel on the counter. "I'm heading to Vivian's. See you back at the station."

———

GINNIE RUSHED BACKSTAGE after the first show with the rest of the chorus girls and did a quick change from her little jitterbug skirt into her gown. She'd almost screwed up one of the routines again. But not because she'd been drinking. After catching sight of Joey in the audience, Ginnie had started

203

thinking about their quickie in the dealers' break room. God, that was good, she'd thought, and her legs went weak, right in the middle of *The Dance of the Veils*.

Ginnie walked around the gaming room a few times, looking for Joey, and was thinking of heading for the bar, when she saw a couple of women staring at her feet. She looked down and realized she'd forgotten to change out of her scuffed dancing shoes. Ginnie didn't care.

Where was Joey?

She hitched up the long skirt of her gown and hurried towards the exit. When an attractive, gray-haired gentleman at one of the roulette tables gave her a smile, she flashed one back, but didn't stop to latch onto his arm and entertain him with her sparkling wit, like she was supposed to.

Ginnie wound her way through the groups of customers crowding the night club—the place was packed. Her breath quickened as she walked past the room where she and Joey had last come together.

As she moved across the lobby outside the Caravan Room, she stopped here and there, stretching up on tiptoes to look over the heads of the people milling about.

There he was. Finally. Talking to his mother over by the bar.

Ginnie moved towards where mother and son stood. She let go of her gown, smoothed it down with her fingers and tried to compose herself. As she neared them, Ginnie tilted her chin up a little higher, locked her eyes on Joey, and added a swing to her hips. *No.* She stopped herself. *Better wait until mama leaves.*

Ginnie hung back where they couldn't see her, but she could still hear their conversation.

"But I want you to stay here tonight, Joey," mama said.

"I need some air," Joey said.

"You can hang your head out the front door and get air. You don't have to leave."

"I need to go out."

"Where? What're you up to?"

Joey looked away from her, frustrated.

"Where you going, Joey?"

Joey swung back to face her. "You really need to know? Okay, I'll tell ya. I'm going to Sophie's. *There!* Feel better, Mom?"

Ginnie felt like Joey had taken a knife and stabbed it right through her heart. She turned and ran. She didn't want to hear anything else.

———

LOGBOOK ENTRY:

I WAITED UNTIL I heard Bruno and his stooges leave before opening my eyes. I sat up and rested my head against the brick wall behind me. Once I'd realized they had me, I figured the only way out was to convince them I was beaten. So I played it like I was on the ropes and hoped Bruno'd be convinced he was giving me the whipping of my life.

A good thing I could take shots to my gut and knew how to roll with a punch, because Bruno meant business. Even so, my face was sore and I could taste blood. Bruno hadn't changed much—technically he might have been 4-F, but his punches weren't. And neither was the whack I got from his buddy's blackjack.

As I got to my feet, using the wall to steady myself, two guys with their dates walked by. The gals cringed and looked away from me. The fellas shook their heads, probably mistaking me for being drunk.

I pulled out a handkerchief, dabbed my lips and cheeks, and gingerly placed the bloodied rag on the spot on my head that was growing lumpier by the second. No blood there, but it was really tender. I found my hat a dozen feet away. It was stepped on and battered, looking pretty much the way I figured my face did.

I was right. When I finally reached the car and checked myself in the rear view mirror, I saw my bottom lip was split open and my cheeks looked like they'd been clawed at by an alley cat. I was going to have a good shiner, too. Hell, no way I was going over the river and letting my old man see me with *this* face.

I didn't really want to show up at The Oasis looking like this either, but I knew no one would be at the house and I couldn't get in without breaking windows. So I drove to the club, hoping I could slip in unnoticed and get keys from Joey.

It was sometime after ten P.M. when I got there. The place sure was jumping. I parked the DeSoto in its usual spot by the back door. Hadn't noticed before, but that door only opened from the inside. So, trying not to feel too self-conscious, I walked around to the front and entered the club's foyer. Yeah, I got looks from the tuxedoed gents and their chichi women.

I smiled back with my fat lip.

"Nick!" Pearl came rushing up to me, a look of alarm on her face. "What happened to you? Are you all right?" She gently took my arm and steered me out of the foyer to a quiet corner.

"I look worse than I feel. I'm okay, really."

Pearl narrowed her eyes as she took stock of the damage to my face. "Who did this?" Sounded like she already knew.

"Bruno Carpella."

"How dare they drag you into this," Pearl said through clenched teeth. "I'll get Doc to patch you up."

She was being protective. I liked that.

"I'm worried Joey's going to come back looking like this, too."

"Why?" I asked. "Isn't he here?"

"He just took off. A few minutes ago. He said he was going to Sophie's—but I didn't believe him, so I sent Hunch after him. I think Joey's gone to the Merchant's Club looking for trouble."

"I'll go, too. I know how to talk to him—I've saved his butt a couple of times."

"But you're in no shape to—"

I didn't waste another second, and sprinted through the foyer and out the door.

———

"WHERE THE FUCK IS LESTER?"

Jimmy the Shiv was not happy. He'd spent the entire day waiting at the Merchants Club. Okay, not exactly—he killed an hour or so in the arms of a beautiful babe. But dammit, Lester must have fallen off the face of the earth for him not to show up. And if he wasn't dead, why wasn't he telling his secretary where he was?

Jimmy looked at his watch. Ten-thirty. He took another swallow of scotch. Rubbed his nose. Shifted around in his chair—his butt itched.

"Goddammit, boys," Jimmy said to both his driver and his bodyguard, "something about this stinks."

———

LOGBOOK ENTRY:

I FLOORED THE DESOTO. It didn't exactly fly like a bat out of hell.

For a dark country road, there was a lot of traffic at that time of night going back and forth between Newport and The Oasis and the Primrose. I must have passed Joey earlier, on my way to The Oasis, but his Cadillac would have been just another set of headlights in the string of lights winding through the hills.

Several times, I managed to squeeze around slower moving vehicles in front of me and get back into my lane just in time to avoid slamming into a car coming from the opposite direction.

Within ten minutes, I was back on Fourth Street—but on the other side of Newport—looking for the Cadillac. It wasn't hard to find, Joey had double parked right in front of the Merchants Club.

I pulled up behind and saw him outside the entrance to the club having words with Hunch. Joey was obviously upset—chopping at the air with his arms and shouting at Hunch who was trying to block his path.

The door to the club opened, and a fella wearing a blue pinstriped suit and a fedora stepped out. Two other big bruisers were right behind him.

Joey elbowed Hunch out of the way. "Hey, Jimmy. Jimmy Turelli."

The man in the fedora stopped and frowned at Joey.

By this time, I'd reached my buddy's side and put a hand on his shoulder. "C'mon, Joey. Let's go."

I startled him. He threw me a surprised look over his

shoulder, but quickly trained his eyes back on the man he'd called Jimmy.

"You don't know me, Turelli, but you know my family. The name's Joey Jules—"

"Oh, yeah," Turelli said, the wariness in his eyes changing over to curiosity, "you look like your father. How's he doin'?"

"Don't bullshit me. You know damn well he's in the hospital."

"Yeah, I was real sorry to hear about it. I hope he's improving."

"I don't believe you give a shit what happens to him. But I do. And I'm warning you, I gotta go back to base in a couple of days, but if anything more happens to my family— if my dad dies or has an 'accident' or anything happens to my mother—I'm coming back. Even if the Navy's shipped me off to Tokyo, I'll fuckin' swim back, track you down, and—" Joey reached in under his jacket and drew out his gun "—personally put all seven slugs right between your fuckin' eyes."

Joey pointed his automatic at Turelli's head. Turelli's bruisers pulled theirs and aimed at Joey. Hunch had his out, too. It was a Mexican stand-off.

Turelli slowly raised his hands. "Hey, now. Let's not get excited, fellas. Let's all put our guns away. We can talk about this."

Turelli's friends waited to see what Joey and Hunch did.

I held my breath and felt a trickle of sweat run down my temple.

Finally, Joey cocked his wrist, pointing the gun up in the air, then slowly put it back into his shoulder holster. Hunch followed suit.

209

Turelli motioned to his boys with a jerk of his head, and they put theirs away. "I understand how upset you are, Joey. You're distraught over what has happened to your father, so I'm excusing you this one time. Your mother and I go back a long way—your father, too. We were partners and I used to go with your mother. I really had the hots for her in a big way. Did you know that, Joey? You could've been my son. So, I'm forgiving you. See, I'm not exactly hard-hearted. But—" he slashed the air with his blunt forefinger, "don't you *ever* come at me like this again."

I was watching Joey and could see his shoulders tense at Turelli's comment about his mother. Another jerk of his shoulder flagged what he was going to do next. I caught Joey's arm and stopped him from throwing a punch at Turelli. Hunch grabbed his other arm. We dragged him to the Cadillac and shoved him into the driver's seat.

I said, "Joey, you're going to calm down and drive back to The Oasis."

"We'll be on your tail all the way," added Hunch.

Joey waved us away. "Yeah, yeah, okay. I'm fine. I did what I came to do. Shit, Nick, what the hell happened to your face?"

"Later," I said, and slammed the door of the Cadillac shut and walked to the DeSoto.

Turelli called out to me. "Better keep a leash on that boy. He's got his momma's temper, but not her brains."

Could be, I thought, and got into the driver's seat.

We all backed away into our respective corners—Turelli and his boys into the Merchants Club; Hunch, Joey, and me to The Oasis.

21

SEPTEMBER 21

"I TOLD YOU," Ducker said, putting his feet up on his desk. "No madam's gonna tell you who their johns are."

Pope yawned and looked at the wall clock in the detective's squadroom. It was 12:30 AM. A couple of days ago, he'd have been in bed by now. Getting used to a new shift was a pain, and he was damn tired after visiting the last three spots on the list by himself. But he wasn't going to admit that their tour of the area's disorderly houses was a waste of time and energy. "Hey, it was *your* idea to begin with that Pearl Jules might've been pissed off at Carl for playing around. At least

211

I'm trying to follow through. Find out who his playmates might be."

Ducker stared at his shoes. "Okay, Dick Tracy, try this one on for size. Maybe Carl Jules had family troubles, but not with his wife. You met his son Joey—kind of a hot head, don't you think? Wops are always fighting amongst themselves. Vendettas. Bad blood. Who knows? Maybe Joey and Dear Old Dad argued that night over something stupid. They're out there in the middle of nowhere in a dark parking lot. Nobody else around. Bang! Bang!"

Pope recalled Joey Jules' display of temper. Maybe the son was covering up his own guilt by making sure the cops knew how "upset" he was over the shooting. Of course, Joey might have been upset he didn't do it properly.

Pope decided to take another look at the statement Joey had given a few hours after the shooting. He opened the file on his desk and started reading. "Nothing here jumps out at me. Left his father to close up the club by himself. He picked up his pal at Union Terminal. Went home. Made a few phone calls. Found out what happened, and then went to the hospital."

Ducker piped up. "We're still just taking Joey's word Carl was alive when he left."

Pope yawned again. "I need another coffee. You?"

"Yeah. Get some donuts, too."

Pope stepped into the corridor and headed towards the desk sergeant to tell him to call the deli. He was halfway down the hall when he saw two men in business suits, who had just entered the station, approach the sergeant.

"Can I help you gentlemen?" the sergeant asked.

"I am Assistant Attorney General Jesse K. Lewis," one man said, "and this is Charles E. Lester, Attorney at Law. I need to speak to the lieutenant in charge." The authoritative voice rang out down the empty tiled hallway.

"Sir?" The sergeant sounded confused.

So was Pope. What were these guys doing here at twelve-thirty in the morning?

"Where's the lieutenant?" Lewis asked.

The sergeant pointed towards Pope. "Uh...well, Acting Chief George Gugel's office is just past that guy and to the left."

The two men, Lewis and Lester, marched down the hall towards Pope, who indicated to them which office was Gugel's. They continued marching right in without knocking.

Pope heard them introduce themselves again, this time to a bewildered-sounding Gugel. He tiptoed nearer to the open door so he could eavesdrop.

Lewis said, "We have a temporary restraining order, signed by Mason Circuit Judge C. D. Newell, enjoining named gamblers from operating, and enjoining the named public officials to stop nonenforcement of the law, and directing the seizure of gambling equipment for presentation to the Campbell Circuit Court as evidence."

There was a brief period of silence. Pope assumed Gugel was reading the document.

Gugel spoke up. "Now? You want me to raid all these clubs this very minute?"

"Yes," Lewis replied.

———

PEARL STOOD BY the reservation desk outside the Caravan Room, and watched the show going on inside. Doc Miller and the band had never sounded better. But one of the chorus girls, Ginnie, was dancing like she wasn't sure of the routine and

213

had completely forgotten how to smile. Where was that girl's mind? Pearl was going to have to talk to the dance captain tomorrow about her. And what was that business earlier on with Joey—calling him over to talk to him? Pearl didn't like the girl.

The crowd was laughing and drinking. Everybody was having a great time. Pearl watched Joey move from table to table, making sure each customer felt like a special guest.

Her heart filled with a mixture of pride and sadness. Joey was a natural. He instinctively knew who to greet and how to talk to them. Like the judge at table 35. Joey flirted with his wife just enough to make her giggle and the judge see himself as some kind of a stud, but not so much that he offended either of them.

Pearl smiled to herself, though she felt sad. In a few days, Joey would be returning to base. She prayed they'd be able to patch things up before he left. Still upset about their earlier confrontation at home, she had watched the rift between them grow even wider when Hunch and Nick brought him back to the club.

Pearl knew Joey had lied to her about going to Sophie's as soon as he opened his mouth and said, "Ma, tell me Jimmy the Shiv is lying. You were never with that fag."

"What about the lying you're doing to me?" She'd wanted to smack him across the face right there in the foyer, and if they'd been anywhere else but the club, she would have. But not there. Not with everyone's eyes on her. She had to keep it together—couldn't give the impression she was falling apart. Pearl held back, clenching her fist tight. "Joey, I told you not to go looking for trouble."

"But is it true or not—you and Jimmy?"

"I can't go into all that right now. There's too much to explain. We'll talk at home, later on." That was a couple of hours earlier, and she hadn't spoken to him since.

As Pearl continued to watch, a man at table 38 called Joey over. The photo girl had her camera pointed at the party at the table and was ready to take a commemorative snapshot. Joey was invited to be included with the revelers.

After the picture was taken, Joey looked up in Pearl's direction, smiled at her, and winked. He's going to break lots of girls' hearts, she thought.

Joey moved towards the back of the room where Nick stood by himself. Doc Miller had done the best he could to clean up Nick's face, but he was still a sight with a bandage over one eyebrow and a few more on his chin and cheeks.

Joey and Nick spoke a few words to each other, then they turned and walked towards Pearl.

———

CLAUDETTE SAT CROSS-LEGGED, wrapped in her silk robe, on the hassock in front of her open bedroom window. She smoked a cigarette and listened to Millie's high-pitched voice come through the thin wall between their rooms. Guess she was entertaining that banker who could only get a hard-on if Millie used baby talk.

"And is Little Peter happy to see me," Claudette mimicked.

She took another deep drag on her cigarette and blew out a long stream of smoke. She was confused. Never before had the cards been so unclear. Who was The Fool pointing to?

Jimmy Turelli sure looked like the one who could open doors for her. He was the big shot. Asked her if she ever thought of trying to get into the movies. Even told her a couple of producers in Hollywood owed him favors. Did that mean he could get her a screen test? "Maybe," Jimmy had said, "if you're a good girl."

But then there was Nick. Claudette always went on instincts and feelings about people. She had a strong feeling about that sailor. Sure, he was nothing much now, but she'd sensed a restlessness and drive inside him. He might go places. And he was a lot better looking than Jimmy Turelli.

Two police cars screeched to a halt in front of the Glenn Rendezvous across the street.

"Well, well. What do we have here?" Claudette said, flicking an ash out the window.

Several uniformed cops jumped out of their cars. One yelled across to another, "We're gonna get 'em all tonight."

Claudette watched them enter the club. She flicked her cigarette butt out into the street, slid off the hassock, and started for the stairs. She wasn't sure what the cop meant by "getting 'em all," but just in case The Oasis was on their hit list, she figured she'd make a telephone call. Warn Joey Jules. It would be a way of repaying him for riding to her rescue.

———

HALF THE CROWD was on the dance floor, the other half sat transfixed by Tweety's saxophone solo.

Pearl stood in the entrance way of the Caravan Room, Joey and Nick at her side.

"Brother," Joey said, "listen to that scrawny little guy, he sure can blow that thing. I never heard him let loose like that."

Nick said, "Yeah, he's hot."

Pearl watched the dancing couples and tried to swallow the lump forming in her throat. If Carl was here, he'd be coaxing her out onto the dance floor. Are we ever going to do that again? she wondered.

Pearl was startled by the sudden ringing of the phone at the reservation desk beside her. The dining room steward picked it up.

"The Oasis. Good evening, can I help you?" He listened for a moment. "Joey Jules? Just a moment, he's standing right here."

The steward held out the phone. "Joey. It's for you."

Pearl stepped aside, shooting her son a quizzical look. He returned the look and grabbed the receiver.

"Yes?" Joey asked.

Pearl studied his face as he listened to the person on the other end. She saw his eyebrows shoot up in surprise. Joey looked up at her. "It's a raid." He turned back to the receiver, said, "Thanks, Claudette, you're a doll," and hung up.

"Who the hell's Claudette?" Pearl asked. Tip-offs on police raids always came from the cops themselves.

"Never mind that right now," Joey said. "She saw them hit the Glenn Rendezvous, heard they were going after other clubs, and—"

Pearl pressed the alarm buzzer on the underside of the reservation desk before Joey finished his sentence.

———

LOGBOOK ENTRY:

YOU COULDN'T MISS the alarm. It was so loud, it hurt. The customers in the Caravan Room covered their ears. Waiters and security men sprinted past me on their way to the gaming room. Joey had already gone, he'd moved so fast.

The lookout man came running up to Pearl. "What's going on. I didn't set it off. Nobody's coming up the road."

Pearl waved him back. "Stay at your post and keep an eye out. We got a tip. They're coming."

The alarm finally stopped. Pearl stepped into the hubbub of the Caravan Room and waved towards the stage.

Doc Miller nodded back to her and then spoke into the microphone. "Ladies and Gentlemen, your attention to the back of the room, please."

The excited chattering in the room quickly died down.

All eyes focused on Pearl. In a calm voice, she said, "No need to panic, folks. We are expecting some policemen to visit us in a few minutes, but we have everything under control. Just go on enjoying yourselves. Doc, keep playing."

I was missing the real action. I ran to the gaming room. All the gamblers had been ushered out, but I was let in seconds before the massive doors were shut and bolted from the inside, just as I'd imagined they would be. The barricade was going to buy a lot of extra time.

I was amazed. It was like a fire drill aboard a battleship. Everyone moved with a purpose. Money boxes and chips were being scooped up by the dealers and pit bosses and taken to the cashier, who was shoving it all into a wall safe. Waiters carted the roulette wheels over to the wall of slot machines. The felt gambling surfaces were taken off the roulette and blackjack tables. Security men lifted the tops of the crap tables and turned them upside down. All the gambling surfaces had been set on top of regulation pool tables.

Over by the slot machines, Joey and Hunch were helping stack the gambling surfaces and roulette wheels up against the slots. When they were finished stacking, Joey moved to the side wall, bent down and pressed his fingers on a section of the baseboard. Paneling slowly dropped out of the ceiling, hiding everything behind a false wall.

In three and a half minutes, the room had been transformed into a billiards parlor.

Joey said, "Okay. Open 'em up."

"Just a second," the cashier shouted. He finished hammering a panel back on the wall, covering up the safe. I was impressed. Even knowing all that stuff was hidden in the walls, I couldn't point out anything that looked suspicious.

When the doors were swung open, the first one in was Pearl. "They're pulling up in front."

22

Bruno was dumbfounded. "What the fuck's going on?" he shouted to Detectives Pope and Ducker who, along with three uniformed patrolmen, had followed some self-righteous looking big shot in a cheap gray suit into the Yorkshire Club.

And what was that shyster lawyer, Charles Lester, doing tagging along?

Bruno tried to catch Ducker's eye as the seven men marched through the restaurant area, right past him, and into the casino. Ducker ignored him.

"Hey! What gives?" Bruno shouted at his back. Ducker was on the pad—Bruno had just seen the guy get his regular pay-off from the Yorkshire Club a few days ago.

"It's a fuckin' raid," Al said.

Manny cursed under his breath.

The customers, the bartenders, the waiters, everybody stopped what they were doing and stared, too shocked to say anything.

Bruno stomped over to the raiders. "You can't go in there. It's a private party."

"Yeah, sure," Pope said, "and you're the birthday boy."

Bruno felt like the rug had been pulled out from under him. The Yorkshire Club was paying Gugel big time, so what was this? And no warning?

The big shot studied the room for a moment, as if counting the house. Bruno could have told him there were over two hundred men and women at the tables. But he kept his mouth shut.

Gray Suit took a few steps forward and waved a piece of paper. "This establishment is closed until further notice. Leave everything where it is. We're seizing the contents of this room under court order."

And there was nothing Bruno could do about it.

BRUNO STOOD FUMING outside the Yorkshire Club. He watched the uniformed cops smoke their cigarettes and joke while they stood guard, waiting for that damn Gugel to arrive with a moving truck to haul away the dice, roulette, and blackjack tables.

Nobody was arrested, but so what? The thing eating away at Bruno's stomach was the double-cross.

Word about the raid had quickly spread around town and across the Licking River to Covington. Everything was shut down tight. Bruno himself was on the phone warning a pal of his at the Flamingo within three minutes of the raiders storming into the Yorkshire. Turned out the leader, Gray Suit, was the goddamn Assistant Attorney General.

Shit, it was a real commando operation. Not only did the Yorkshire get hit, so did the Merchants Club, the Beverly Hills, the York Tavern, the Glenn Rendezvous, and The Oasis. All at once. And nobody had any idea it was in the works.

Bruno pulled out a pack of cigarettes, tapped one out on his wrist, and lit up. No sense sticking around—it was a waste of time—wasn't gonna put any money in his pocket.

Bruno caught Lester's eye as the lawyer came out of the club. Lester turned away. That boiled his blood. Who the hell did Lester think he was? Made Bruno want to take that goddamn mouthpiece and work him over—or anyone else, for that matter, who'd gone back on a deal.

Bruno had the itch to bust someone's head. He turned on his heels. It was time to go calling on welshers who owed him money.

———

GINNIE BRAKED AS she went round a bend in the road, trying to find her way in the dark. The car veered from side to side. She'd been taking swigs from her flask of bourbon all night and was having a little trouble controlling things. Ginnie gripped the steering wheel and tried to aim the headlights down the center of the road. Without any moonlight, it was hard to see the edge and she was afraid of going off and slamming into a tree or rolling over into a gully.

All she knew about the raid back at The Oasis was that the alarm buzzer went off, and her drinking was interrupted by a uniformed cop poking his head into the dancers' dressing room.

When she'd asked the cop what he was looking for and he replied, "Slots," she'd heard, "Sluts" through her drunken haze, and shot back, "Ya gotta go to Sophie's for them."

The cop had given her a puzzled look and walked away, shaking his head.

Ginnie laughed to herself, thinking about it now. It would serve Joey right to be thrown into jail. But she was glad the cops left without finding any evidence of gambling, because she still had unfinished business with him.

Slots or sluts, it was all the same to Joey. That's all he wanted—things to play with. The self-centered bastard didn't give a damn about love. Ginnie had waited more than a year for him to come back, had saved herself just for him, and now here he was treating her like shit. How dare he go to Sophie's for a fuck after they'd made love just a few hours earlier.

Ginnie slowed the car again, and looked out the side window. Yeah, it was somewhere around here.

Squinting into the darkness, she found the spot of level ground where she'd pulled off once before. Ginnie wrenched the steering wheel hard to the right, until she felt the car bump off the road. Then she stamped on the brakes, bringing the car to a lurching halt.

"God, you can't see a blessed thing out there." She yanked open the glove compartment, took out a flashlight, and got out of the car.

All she could see in the beam of her flash were thick bushes.

"There was a clearing somewhere. Where the hell was I? Maybe over there."

Three steps off the road, the prickly branches snagged Ginnie's short skirt and scratched her legs. The heel of her dance shoe sank down into two inches of mud. "Shit!" Ginnie shouted. "I should've changed out of this stupid jitterbug costume."

———

ON STAGE IN THE Caravan Room, Raymond Twitty was taking his time packing away his saxophone and music. The police had finished searching The Oasis from top to bottom and retreated, grumbling and empty-handed. The staff, except for security, had been sent home. But Raymond had decided to hang back. This was the night.

Just then, he noticed Pearl and Joey walk into the bar.

———

LOGBOOK ENTRY:

IT HAD BEEN one helluva day. Guess I looked kind of bushed, because Pearl offered me her keys to the house.

"You go on ahead," she told me. "Joey and I still have to go over the day's receipts."

I said, "Thanks, but I can wait." I had been camped out

in the booth at the far end of the bar ever since the cops chased the customers out and went on their little safari throughout The Oasis, looking for a big catch. To tell the truth, I was too tired and too comfortable to drive myself anywhere.

I told Joey and Pearl, "I'll just wait here until you're finished," and pulled out my pipe. They walked away.

Then things started happening.

I was packing my pipe and getting ready to light it, when I saw Tweety hurry out of the Caravan Room, through the bar, out towards the lobby. He stood just outside the bar and watched Joey and Pearl go up the stairs. Then the little guy, looking nervous as hell, ran into the men's room.

———

RAYMOND TWITTY OPENED the door of the men's room just a crack and peeked out. It was 3:00 A.M. and the lobby was quiet. Countless times over the past half hour, he'd looked out into the lobby, waiting for his opportunity.

Finally, Raymond heard footsteps coming down the staircase. He held his breath, waiting for whoever it was to come into view.

It was Joey.

Raymond watched him go into the gaming room.

Pearl was alone upstairs.

———

PEARL WAS HAVING trouble concentrating. After counting the night's receipts, Joey had gone downstairs to help Hunch close up, leaving her alone to make out the bank deposit. But she kept making mistakes. She started filling out a new slip, and found herself making the same mistakes all over again.

Pearl groaned, threw down her pen, and pinched the bridge of her nose. Oh God, she thought. There'd just been too many things to deal with that day. First, Jimmy Turelli showing up—at Carl's bedside, no less. Then the arguments with Joey. *And* Nick coming back with a punched-in face.

She made the sign of the cross and, fingering the gold crucifix around her neck, whispered a prayer to the Blessed Virgin Mary. "Thank you for bringing my Peppino, my little Joey, back before his temper got him killed tonight. And thank you for the warning about the raid—I don't care that you used a whore. But tell me, why didn't the damn cops tip us off? Carl and I have been paying them all these years. *What happened? Do they suddenly want more money? Are they getting greedy?"

———

RAYMOND FELT A twinge of anxiety in the pit of his stomach. He had to take this chance. It was now or never.

Raymond gulped air and pulled open the door.

———

LOGBOOK ENTRY:

TWEETY HAD BEEN in the men's room for close to half an hour. I was just starting to think I should go check on the little fella to see if he needed help, when Joey came downstairs and went into the gaming room. A second later, Tweety bolted out and crossed the lobby to the staircase, where he paused for a moment, looking up.

Pearl was up there by herself. I didn't like the look of things. Whatever exhaustion I'd been feeling disappeared. A surge of adrenaline charged me up, and I jumped to my feet. By the time I reached the lobby, Tweety was up the stairs.

I started to follow, but held back as I saw him stop just outside Pearl's office.

———

JUST AS PEARL finished her prayer, she became aware of someone at the door.

"Excuse me, Pearl."

She looked up. It was Raymond Twitty, the saxophone player. He looked a little stranger than usual, she thought. His wispy hair was plastered across his forehead with sweat and his eyes darted around the room. He should have already gone home. Maybe he was sick. Pearl managed a half-hearted smile. "Raymond? What can I—"

"Pearl," Raymond said, his voice cracking.

"Yes?"

Raymond cleared his throat. "Um, I must talk to you." He stepped into the office and pushed the door behind him, not quite shutting it.

"What's the problem?" Pearl asked.

Raymond took another step towards her. "Oh, there's no problem. I'm here for you."

"Here for me?" *What the hell's he talking about?*

"I can't stand it anymore, watching you try to handle all this by yourself."

"Thank you for being concerned, but I'm—"

"You may want us all to think you're a strong woman, but I know how you feel deep inside."

Pearl frowned at him. *What?*

"Oh," Raymond said, looking up at the ceiling, "you can find lots of men who will come and help you run The Oasis. Even your own son Joey can do that." He looked back at Pearl. "But you need more than a strong right arm. You need arms to hold you. You have far greater needs that aren't being satisfied."

"Raymond, I—"

"No, wait, let me finish. Over these last two years, I've seen you look at me. Those secret looks were so important to me. It was like we had our own communication, our own silent language. Just our hearts were talking and nobody could hear. But now, we don't have to worry about what people will think. You and I can be together. Finally, out in the open. *Oh, Pearl, I love you—*"

Pearl burst out laughing. "Oh, Tweety, where did you ever get *that* idea?"

"Pearl . . . don't play with me like this. I'm giving you my heart, I—"

Pearl couldn't stand it anymore. "Get *out* of here!"

———

LOGBOOK ENTRY:

I HEARD IT ALL, every word. Tweety burst out of Pearl's office. He spat out "Bitch!" and stormed past me.

There was a part of me that wanted to go in there and tell her I had the hots for her, too, but Tweety was acting weird, and I didn't like the look in his eyes. So I followed him. Down the stairs. Through the lobby. Through the gaming room, which was empty. And out the back door—no time to find Joey and tell him what I was doing. I kept my distance and made sure Tweety didn't know I was shadowing him. It took a while for him to walk across the parking lot and reach his car. In the meantime, I got behind the wheel of the DeSoto and waited.

A couple of years ago, I'd known a sailor who was fixated on a singer in a bar in Shanghai, just like Tweety was with Pearl. When the singer brushed him off, the sailor slit her throat then torched the bar, burning it to the ground. That's why I had to follow Tweety—the guy had just been humiliated, and I had the image of The Oasis going up in flames.

The possibility grew the more I thought about it. Maybe my imagination was running wild again, but I *had* seen Tweety and Bruno talking like old pals on that street corner a couple of days earlier. And it was Bruno's job to intimidate Pearl—what better way to scare her into giving up than to set her place on fire. It didn't make sense to torch a club you wanted to take over, but that was the crazy way they did business in Little Mexico. The Cleveland Syndicate had burned down that other casino—what was it, The Beverly Hills?—to get Pete Schmidt to sell out.

Tweety could be thinking "I'll get back at her. I'll go find Bruno and tell him 'Let's burn it down.'" Yeah, it all made sense. To me at least. Tweety didn't look pathetic anymore—he looked downright dangerous.

I watched his car pull away from its parking spot, cross the lot, and turn onto the drive. Even though Tweety was driving a piece of junk, he was moving pretty fast. I shifted into gear and stamped on the gas, almost stalling the engine. I lurched out of the lot after him.

It was easy to hang back a ways and still keep track of Tweety, because nobody else was traveling up or down Route 9. Or so I thought.

As we rounded a bend, I was surprised to see the headlights of another car pulled over to the side of the road. Nobody was standing beside it, trying to wave me down. Could've been a couple in the back seat grabbing some nooky. But with their lights on? Hell, if anyone needed help, they were going to have to wait for the next guy. Up ahead, Tweety's rear lights were disappearing fast. I was losing ground.

I pressed down on the gas pedal.

———

GINNIE LAID THE FLASHLIGHT on the ground and crawled through the underbrush on her hands and knees. Mosquitoes buzzed around her head and nailed themselves to her arms and legs. She swatted at them, but it was a wasted effort—there were just too many. Gritting her teeth, she patted the ground in front of her. Nothing. Ginnie picked up the flashlight and moved forward a few feet, then laid it back down again. The grass was higher here. Her knees felt wet, and she realized she was crawling into a boggy area.

"I couldn't have thrown it much farther than *this*. It's gotta be here."

Ginnie picked up the flashlight and shone it around. She heard a car coming, and switched it off. Even though she was a good thirty feet away from the road, she held her breath. *Oh, shit. I should've turned off the headlights. Keep driving.*

The car sped by.

Ginnie breathed again and flicked away a mosquito that had been sucking on her cheek. She was about to turn her flashlight back on, when she heard a second car coming from the same direction. This one slowed a little.

I don't want help. Don't stop.

It picked up speed and kept on going, as if the driver had heard her.

Ginnie let out her breath, clicked the light back on, and stood up. She swayed a little, took a step backwards to try to keep her balance, but stumbled and fell. Dizzy and confused, she shone the flashlight around to get her bearings, and realized she was facing the road. The beam of light bounced off metal about ten feet away.

There. It was back closer to the road. Ginnie knew she couldn't throw farther than that. She pushed through the underbrush, picked up the gun, and hurried back to the car.

23

RAYMOND UNLOCKED THE door of his apartment. It was only then he realized he'd left his saxophone at the club.

"Aw, fuck! I don't want to go back to that place."

He kicked the door open, went in, and switched on the overhead light.

"Why do I need my fuckin' saxophone? I'm not going to play it anymore. I'm not going to do *any*thing anymore."

Raymond went over to the green painted dresser and started ripping the photos off the mirror.

"Bitch!" he yelled, each time he removed one and

threw it on the floor. "Bitch! Bitch!"

Raymond stopped and looked in the mirror, leaning in until he was nose-to-nose with himself.

"Oh, Pearl," he said, swooning, "I love you."

He pushed away and sneered at his reflection. "You goddamn pathetic little piece of shit."

Raymond focused his sneer at the limp geranium in the little crystal vase he'd placed in front of the mirror that morning.

He balled up his fist and swung at the vase, sending it across the room where it shattered against the wall.

Raymond walked over to the dead geranium, stamped on it with his heel and smeared it into the wood floor.

Air. He needed air.

The window fought him, sticking every half inch. Raymond cursed loudly and yanked at the wood frame until he finally got it open. A street light illuminated the row of carefully tended pink geraniums on the fire escape. They were all lined up, sitting in their clay pots and smiling at him. Mocking him.

Raymond lunged forward, out the window, and batted at them with his forearms, pushing two of the pots through the railings. They smashed on the concrete below.

Even with the window wide open, Raymond's apartment felt like an airless coffin. He had to get out of there. Move around. Take a walk. *Yeah, that's a good idea.*

Raymond slammed the door on his way out and didn't bother to lock it.

LOGBOOK ENTRY:

THE CLUNKER I was driving was in better shape than Tweety's old jalopy. I was able to catch up and follow him through the empty streets of Newport. No action going on inside any of the clubs I passed; even their neon signs were switched off. Guess the rumor was true—the cops had raided everybody.

Tweety parked in front of a squat brick apartment building and stormed from his car. I slowed, waiting to see what he would do next.

He entered the front door of the building. Was Tweety just going home? I didn't know if this was where he lived. Maybe he was meeting someone.

I pulled up behind his car and cut my engine. From where I sat, I had a good view of the front of the building, and could see part way down an alley that ran between it and the dilapidated apartment building next door. There were rusty fire escapes attached to the side wall at every other window. Clotheslines stretched across the alley like thick cobwebs.

A light came on in a second floor window part way down the alley. Had to be Tweety's. I noticed the row of flowerpots on the fire escape. He sure was an odd egg.

Nothing else happened for a few minutes. I just watched. Suddenly, Tweety appeared at the window and yanked it open with great difficulty, cursing loudly the whole time.

He seemed to gaze at his little garden for a half minute, then surprised me by leaning out the window and delivering a quick one-two, knocking a couple of flower pots off the fire escape.

That was definitely odd.

Not long after that, Tweety reappeared at the front door of the building and headed in my direction, eyes locked on the pavement in front of him. Quickly tilting my hat to cover my face, I lay down across the front seat, but he didn't get into his car like I expected. His footsteps clicked along the sidewalk right beside me as he passed my car. When I figured he was far enough away, I popped halfway up and peered over the back of the driver's seat.

Tweety was almost at the corner. I noticed someone walking towards him—a guy, a lot bigger than Tweety. The two met under a streetlight.

It was Bruno Carpella.

They exchanged a few words, but I couldn't make out what they were saying. Bruno threw an arm around Tweety's shoulder and squeezed. Hard. They headed back in my direction. I slumped down into my sleeping position. As the two pals walked by, I heard Bruno say something about going upstairs to "have a little discussion about this."

I sure as hell wanted to hear this discussion. As soon as they disappeared into the building, I got out of the car and entered the alley.

The fire escape ladder was low enough for me to jump up and grab the bottom rung. It made a loud clang as it locked into position. I froze for a moment, hoping I hadn't just alerted the whole damn neighborhood to my presence.

Nobody threw open their windows and yelled at me, so, trying not to make any more noise, I hoisted myself up the ladder towards the light coming out of Tweety's apartment.

Just as I landed outside the open window, I heard the two men talking. I took a quick look inside at what appeared to be a one room apartment. Their voices were coming from the hallway on the other side of the partially open door. I flattened myself up against the brick wall and listened.

"But I'm telling you," Tweety said in his high, squeaky voice, "I don't have it."

"Yeah, yeah," Bruno said, "we've all had a shitty night."

It sounded like Bruno used Tweety's body to ram his way into the apartment, making the door crash against the wall. There was a thud. Pretty safe bet Tweety had hit the floor.

"Ha! Watch your step," Bruno said.

"Hey, what gives?" Tweety's voice squeaked even higher.

"I'm sick and tired of you fuckin' around. Now pay up."

"But—but, Bruno. I told you—"

"Yeah, yeah, well you got a saxophone don't ya? Must be worth a lot of dough. You can hock it."

Silence.

"Where the hell's that oversized horn of yours? I thought you slept with it—hey, what's this shit all over the floor?"

"Nothing."

"What nothing? Looks like snapshots of some broad." Bruno's voice was strained, like he was trying to bend over. "This Pearl Jules? Yeah. Damn, she's got some pair of knockers on her, don't she?"

Silence.

Bruno spoke up again. "Got the hots for her, huh, Tweetybird? What do you do, stand in front of her pictures when you get home from work and jack off?"

"I . . ."

Bruno laughed. "So you're the one who shot Carl Jules. Bet the cops would love to get their hands on stuff like this. It's what they call, uh, motive. Yeah, you got a motive. Where's your gun, you pantywaisted—"

"Hey, wait. No. I don't own one. I never shot Carl—I couldn't—I—I was playing cards with a couple of your pals, Manny and Al. They took me for half my week's salary that night. Go ask them."

I imagined Bruno cocking an eyebrow at Tweety. "Yeah . . . Maybe . . . Shit, I don't give a fuck if you did or didn't. I just want the dough you owe me."

"I tell you, I don't have it."

Tweety and Bruno weren't going to be hatching up any plots to burn down The Oasis. This or any night. I was tired of trailing around after losers. Time for me to go home.

I'd started inching my way back to the ladder, when I heard Tweety cry out, *"No, don't!"*

I kept inching. The squirt had it coming to him for playing with a guy like Bruno.

It was the sound of bone snapping and Tweety's cry of pain that kept me from going over the side and down the ladder.

Those old memories of Bruno, the neighborhood bully, pounding on that little colored boy years ago flashed to the front of my mind. Bruno played too rough for me to stand on the sidelines and live with myself.

"Okay, Tweety," Bruno said, "let's work on the other arm."

I doffed my hat and picked up two of the clay flowerpots on the fire escape. Once again, I flattened myself

237

against the brick wall and peered through the window.

Bruno's back was to me. He was laughing, pulling on Tweety's arm. Tweety was screaming his head off. Didn't matter if the neighbors heard the commotion and called the police—Bruno had to be stopped now.

The window was open wide enough for me to crouch and step down into the apartment.

Holding the two flowerpots in front of me, I took three running steps before Bruno turned. He let go of Tweety's arm and reached into his jacket, going for his gun. At the same time, I hauled back with both arms and swung them together, smashing Bruno's ugly face like a ripe melon between both pots.

Blood and dirt and pink petals went flying everywhere.

24

GINNIE PASSED A couple of cars coming out of The Oasis parking lot. She couldn't see the drivers, but neither of the cars were Cadillacs, so she figured there was a chance Joey was still there.

As she drove around to the back and saw the Cadillac in its spot, a mix of anger and anxiety made her hands start to shake. The bastard *had* to be inside The Oasis—she'd seen him driving his father's car all week.

Ginnie pulled up to the back door and cut the engine. She reached across the seat and picked up the gun. Where to put it? Ginnie looked down at the skimpy costume she was wearing and cursed, wishing she'd changed into her street clothes. She fumbled with the lower two buttons of her blouse, finally undoing them, and stuffed the gun in under the skirt's tight waistband. The cold metal cut into her belly. Her hands shook so much, she couldn't button herself up.

I need another drink, she thought, and went for the flask under the seat. Two swigs emptied it. That would have to do. Ginnie struggled again with the buttons until she finally got her blouse done up. She pulled at the fabric, puffing it out over the handle of the gun.

"A little present for you," her precious Joey had said, when he gave her the Beretta. She'd been telling him how nervous she was, driving home from The Oasis late at night, how she didn't feel safe. So he'd given her the gun and spent a few weeks, before he left for Navy boot camp, showing her how to shoot it.

Ginnie got out of the car, and went to the back door of the club. She pulled on the handle. *Damn.* She'd forgotten. It could only be opened from the inside.

She banged on the heavy metal door, her tiny knuckles barely making a sound. "Joey!" Even her voice sounded feeble. Gotta get in, she thought, and began pacing up and down in front of the door. There were still a few cars in the parking lot. Someone had to come out soon. She kicked the door, trying to make a bigger noise. Nobody came.

Ginnie went back to her pacing. A moment later, she heard the latch click. She hurried to the door and took a deep breath, trying to compose herself. It was one of the security guys leaving for the night. He stared at her, puzzled. Ginnie pushed past him with just a hurried "Thanks" and checked to see if Joey was in the gaming room. He wasn't.

She moved quickly towards the lobby.

Someone called her name. Ginnie looked across the lobby to the bar, where the voice had come from. Hunch Williams stared at her. Her palms began to sweat, and she could hear the blood pounding in her ears.

"What're you doing here?" Hunch asked.

"Oh, I forgot something in the dressing room," she said. "I'll just be a minute."

She slipped into the Caravan Room.

Three men were standing by the stage—Joey and two security men.

There's the son of a bitch. This is it.

Joey looked so handsome in his tuxedo. He cocked his head and smiled at one of the security men. Nobody should be allowed to see that smile but me, Ginnie thought. She stuffed down the rage that was ready to explode from deep inside her.

"Joey?" Ginnie called out.

He turned and frowned at her.

"I need to see you," she said, adding a sweetness to her voice.

"Oh, Ginnie—" She heard disgust in the way he almost spat out her name. "You still here? What do you want?"

Joey started towards her. Ginnie steeled herself. *Got to do this right.*

"I've got something to give you," she said.

"What happened to you?" Joey asked when he got closer. "Looks like you've been trying to crawl over a barbed wire fence."

"Never mind that. Come with me."

Joey was standing right in front of her now. He said in

a lowered voice, "If this is another one of your urges for a quickie—I gotta tell you, I'm tired and it's time to go home."

The bastard. Ginnie smiled and took him by the hand. "Well, this can't wait. Don't worry, it won't take long."

She pulled Joey out of the Caravan Room, across the lobby, and into the dealers' break room. He didn't resist.

———

"F INALLY," PEARL SAID ALOUD. She laid down her pen and stuffed the bank deposit into the leather pouch. If I can get through this day, I can get through any day, she thought.

Hunch poked his head into the office.

"I'm almost ready," Pearl said.

"Yeah, well, hate to tell you, but you got another problem."

"I don't want to hear it."

"Okay." Hunch disappeared from the doorway.

"Hunch! Come back here."

The head of security gave Pearl a rare smile.

"What's going on now?"

"Joey's at it again. He's with Ginnie. Saw them go into the dealers' break room."

"Just now?"

"Yeah, a minute ago. Want me to go break it up?"

Pearl stared at her desk, rubbing her temple. "Oh, Jeez . . . Mother of God . . . no . . . I'll do it. I just need to close up here. It'll just take me a minute or two."

———

GINNIE CLOSED THE DOOR. She leaned against it and watched Joey flop down on the sofa where she had made love to him that very afternoon. And the prick *still* ran out to that whorehouse.

Joey stretched out his legs, crossing them at the ankles, and laced his fingers behind his head. "Okay, you've got my attention. What's up?"

Ginnie smiled, took a few steps towards him. She started trying to unbutton her blouse.

"I told you," Joey said, sitting up straight, "it's late, I'm tired, and we're closing up."

"Yeah, so? You were closing up last week when your father and I caught you in here with that blonde. What's the difference?" She managed to get the first button undone.

"Oh, shit. You gonna bring that up again? You don't own me."

"But you promised you'd come back to me after the war. You wanted me to wait for you." Ginnie's fingers fumbled with the second button.

"I never said that."

"You did!" she screamed. "You did, you goddamn lying bastard!"

Joey jumped to his feet. "Ginnie, you're drunk. You're not making sense. Go on home."

He brushed past her and reached for the doorknob.

Ginnie yanked at her blouse, ripping it open and grabbed her gun. "Don't you talk to me like I'm some poor pathetic little girl."

Joey turned the knob and started to pull the door open.

Ginnie held her Beretta steady, the way Joey'd taught her, and aimed at his back. "I made a mistake last week, but I'm not going to make the same one again."

Joey stopped, leaving the door half open. "What're you talkin' about?" He turned and looked over his shoulder at her. "Hey, what the fuck?"

Ginnie's words rushed out. "I shot your father. It was dark. I thought he was you."

"You? *You?*" Joey stared in disbelief.

Tears welled up in Ginnie's eyes and she felt the room start to spin. "I couldn't believe it. You—you screwed that blonde. And after all your promises. I drove around—didn't know what else to do. Finished off a whole flask of bourbon." The gun in her hand was heavy. She lowered her arm. "When I came back here, the DeSoto was the only car in the lot. So I thought *you* were closing up. How the hell was I supposed to know you'd taken your father's Cadillac?"

The door swung wide.

Pearl stood in the opening, her expression a blank.

Ginnie looked from her to Joey, and sobbed. "You're right, Joey. I'm drunk. Again." She breathed in, let it all out in a sigh. "I'm going home now."

Tears spilled out and ran down her cheeks. Ginnie looked back at Pearl and watched her reach into her purse. *What's she doing? Getting me a hanky?*

Pearl extended her arm, offering what she'd pulled out.

Ginnie saw the blast a split second before her left eye was shot out and the .22 slug slammed into her brain.

25

SEPTEMBER 22

CLAUDETTE STEPPED INTO HER new black dress. It was an off-the-shoulder number she'd bought that day with two bills from the roll of twenties Jimmy Turelli had given her the night before. Millie didn't know it yet, but she was going to inherit Claudette's closet full of four dollar dresses.

Sitting in front of the mirror, Claudette piled up her hair and pinned it in place, copying the style she'd seen on Barbara Stanwyck in last week's *Photoplay* spread.

She glanced over her shoulder at the cards laid out on her bed. The Fool had shown up again. Claudette turned back to the mirror and penciled in her eyebrows, her hand trembling a little. It certainly had been an interesting reading. Things were really going to start happening.

The sounds of a car coming to a stop out in front made her glance towards her open window. She listened as car doors slammed and footsteps came up the walk. Claudette took her time to carefully paint her lips red. She heard Sophie's grunts out in the hall as she reached the top of the steps.

There was a knock on the door. "Claudette? Your gentleman caller is here. Don't keep him waiting."

"Be right there." Claudette reached for the little blue bottle of *Evening In Paris*. She was about to spritz herself— No, she thought. Better no smell, than the smell of cheap perfume. Next item on her shopping list was a bottle of something a hell of a lot more expensive.

Claudette posed for herself. "Slick chick," she said to her reflection. One last thing. She went over to her bed and gathered up the Tarot cards. This time, she'd seen a faint resemblance between The Fool's profile and Nick Cavanaugh's. She wrapped her cards up in a silk scarf and put them away in the drawer of her night table.

As Claudette headed downstairs to meet Jimmy the Shiv, she realized this was the first time she was going against what she believed the cards were telling her. But, she thought, business is business and a girl's gotta make a living.

———

Even HAVING A good-looking dame on his arm didn't make Jimmy the Shiv feel any better. He sipped at his wine and glanced across the table at her, sitting beside his bodyguard. What was her name? Clarice? Colette? Claudine? Oh, yeah, Claudette. Yeah, that's what it was. Well, at least she was having a good time.

But Jimmy hadn't come to the Beverly Hills for the floor show and dinner. He had business to talk over with Sam Tucker.

Jimmy looked around the packed Empire Room. Yeah, Tucker was doing a hell of a job running this place. The Beverly made the Yorkshire Club look like a crummy bustout joint. Sam had come over to the table almost as soon as they'd been seated.

Jimmy nodded to his bodyguard. "Take the girl out for a spin on the dance floor. Sam and I gotta talk." Jimmy took a puff on his cigar and watched Claudette's ass wiggle as she was led away.

Sam launched right in. "Look at this crowd, we got close to six hundred people here tonight. That damn raid didn't hurt this part of the business."

"Yeah." Jimmy flicked the ash off his cigar. "Now, about the gambling equipment the cops seized from us. Where do you think it all disappeared to?"

Sam winked. "Funny thing about that. Forty-one slot machines, a bunch of roulette wheels, dice tables—the cops lock up the casino room, put a couple of their own men outside and *Poof!* it's all gone."

"Gee, I'm flabbergasted."

"Yeah, it's a mystery," Sam said, pulling on his earlobe. "Like I told that damn Attorney General Meredith, I was here until nine A.M. and left when the county chief of police left. I don't know what happened after that."

Jimmy rolled his cigar between his lips. "Maybe the

stuff was hijacked from the cops themselves."

"Maybe. That sounds good." Sam nodded his head. "It could be that the officials sent someone over to pick up the equipment. Maybe they got it, or maybe it was taken away from them after they left the club. Makes sense to me, 'cause there's no evidence the club was broken into."

Sam's eyes darkened. "Enough of that. What's this shit with Lester?"

"I don't know. But now I know why I couldn't find him all day yesterday. He must've been in bed with the Attorney General for months getting the paperwork ready for those raids."

"Who didn't get raided?"

"Everyone got hit. But there were a couple of places that must've been warned 'cause when the cops showed, there was nothing for them to take."

"Who?"

"Pete Schmidt's Glenn Rendezvous for one," Jimmy said. "And you know that place has a shitload of equipment. And then there's The Oasis. I mean they're out here in the hills like us, but they got warned. I can't figure that one out. I can see Pete Schmidt cutting a deal with Lester, but hell would have to freeze over before the Jules family would tie themselves to anybody."

Sam stood up from the table. "Did you see that Lester tagging along with the cops last night? He's got balls."

Jimmy laughed. "Yeah, guess we'll have to have a meeting. Get everyone together in Cleveland and decide who gets to chop 'em off."

———

LOGBOOK ENTRY:

THE TRAIN WAS LATE. I had an hour to kill before boarding and starting my three-day trek back to San Diego. Joey had dropped me off at Union Terminal, telling me he'd fly back and meet me at the barracks in a few days. There was still some family business for him to attend to. I guess it probably had to do with the fact his father was still in a coma.

I didn't want to spend the next hour watching all the crying and kissing around me, as gals said goodbye to their husbands and boy friends, so I headed for the newsstand in the concourse. It felt strange being back in my uniform again—seemed longer than a week since I'd last worn it. I'd been immersed in this world of gangsters and gambling and forgotten it was only a temporary situation.

I picked through the various magazines, finally deciding on a copy of the latest *Black Mask*. One of these days, I promised myself, my byline's going to be on the front cover. Three days on the train was the perfect time to start working on the story. Guess I could end it with my hero beating up the villain with a couple of flowerpots, but I'd have to change the victim from a pansy like Tweety into a sexy babe.

"That must've been some battle you were in," the newsdealer said, nodding at my beaten up face. "Hope you're going home, sailor."

"Yep, I am." *You should've seen the other guy.*

I'd left Bruno unconscious in that apartment, and taken Tweety to the hospital to get patched up. As the doctor was putting his broken arm in a cast, Tweety—or Raymond, as he asked me to call him—said he was getting the hell out of

Newport and going to his sister's in Dayton. I asked if he wanted to get the cops involved. Raymond just looked up at me with raised eyebrows, then laughed.

Apparently, while we were in the hospital, Bruno had come to and slunk out into the night to lick his wounds, because when we got back to the apartment he was gone.

I didn't go back to The Oasis, just drove to the house, parked outside, and slept in the front seat of the car until Joey and Pearl came home. Everybody was too tired to care about what the other guy had done that night.

Anyway, I walked around Union Terminal until it was time to board the train. As we pulled out of the station, I looked out the window and said goodbye to Cincinnati. Never did see my own family. It didn't feel right, my being just across the river and not making the effort. So close but, at the same time, so far away. Probably for the best. People don't change. My old man would try to cut me down with his tongue. My mom would cry and my little brother would sit in the corner, looking scared. I'd storm out, pissed off at myself for coming back before I was on top of the world.

Funny how the place that filled me with so much anger and hatred would be right across the river from the place where I had one of the best times of my life. So much for my wanting to stay as far away from Cincinnati as possible.

It was like making a full circle. Almost.

I didn't know if my crossing over and having that family reunion was in the cards.

But I sure as hell was coming back to Little Mexico.

———

STEVE POPE LAY in bed. His pregnant wife, snuggled up beside him, was fast asleep. Shit, they'd never had any secrets between them before this one, and it was pushing him further and further away from her. He felt dirty inside, but he couldn't come clean and tell her what he was going through. Keeping her in the dark was the only way he knew to protect her. Pope pictured the fifty dollar bribe from Pete Schmidt he'd locked away in the safety deposit box, and wondered how much cash Virgil Ducker, Chief Gugel—and God knows who else—had stashed away over the years.

Pope felt just as alone at work. The gulf between him and the rest of the guys on the force widened every day. He would have to be careful of what he said around the station. He'd already made the mistake of voicing his disgust to Virgil. But it turned his stomach the way serious crimes were being committed and nobody was doing a damn thing about it.

Forget the gambling and prostitution—nobody on the force seemed to care who dumped Dandy Charlie in the river or who shot Carl Jules. It was all a game. And the rules were simple: Just look away.

But it made him sick to think about the boys overseas giving their lives to protect his family from those fucking Nazis and Japs and Italians—just that day the newspapers reported Prime Minister Churchill's announcement that a mass invasion of the Continent from the west would begin.

And here he was, sitting on his fat ass doing nothing and collecting money. Dirty money. Could even be blood money.

Pope stared into the darkness. Maybe there *was* something he could do. He got out of bed, put on his robe and went downstairs. He rummaged around in a kitchen drawer and found a small blank notebook.

Pope sat at the table and started writing it all down—everything he knew about what was going on in Little Mexico. Maybe he could turn accepting bribes into a way of getting the goods on those sons of bitches. Maybe he could collect enough evidence against the big shots and pull them all down. Maybe someday honest politicians would get elected to City Hall.

Pope was only halfway down the first page when he stopped and dropped his pencil. Was he crazy? Did he really think he could get away with this? Or was he writing his own death sentence?

———

CARL STAGGERED TOWARDS the door at the far end of a corridor. He didn't think he'd been down it before. Even though it was shorter than the others, his legs were so heavy, he didn't know if he could make it. But he had to—it was the last door. He'd tried all the others.

Carl's lungs strained for air. Something told him all he had to do was open that door and he'd get the air he needed. But it was so hard to get to. Finally, dragging himself, he reached the doorway and stood in front of it. Carl couldn't hold his body up anymore. With a thrust of his shoulders, he threw the full weight of his body against the door.

Carl burst through to the other side.

His eyes popped open.

Light dazzled him.

Through the glare, Carl could see a figure in white standing off in a corner.

"Where the hell am I?" Carl murmured weakly.

The nurse turned from flirting with the security man and rushed to Carl's bedside.

———

PEARL LOCKED THE FRONT DOOR of The Oasis. At last, she thought. She hadn't expected this night to be so busy, what with the news coverage of the raid and the casino area closed. It seemed everybody in Cincinnati suddenly wanted to live dangerously and come over the river to have dinner at a notorious night spot. They had four hundred customers that night—lots of first-timers who "wanted to see where the gambling took place." But Pearl kept the heavy doors to the gaming room locked.

It had been an exhausting night. Still, there was one matter she had to attend to.

Hunch and Joey were waiting for her at the bar. Together they all headed into the kitchen. Joey yanked open the door to the walk-in refrigerator.

The two men went to work on the stack of boxes in the far corner, moving them so they could get to the wooden barrel hidden underneath. They rolled the barrel out of the refrigerator and into the kitchen.

"Where do you want it, Mom?" Joey asked.

"Set it over there." Pearl pointed to a large metal sliding door. "We can roll it down the ramp and load it in the truck."

Hunch and Joey rolled the barrel across the kitchen floor to where she had indicated and turned it upright.

"Open it up, Hunch." Pearl wanted one last look.

He pried the lid off the barrel and undid the burlap sack inside. Joey stuffed his hands in his pockets and turned away from the sight.

Pearl reached into the sack and grabbed a clump of red hair. She yanked the dead girl's head back so she could study her face, the hole where her left eye had been.

Ginnie's other brown eye stared back.

Pearl felt rage burning inside her again. She shook the dead girl's head. *My son deserves better than you, you drunken tramp. Thank God you were so stupid, I could've lost both my men to you. What were you doing, playing some stupid game trying to scare my son? No, more likely you were too drunk—no, too dumb—to realize there weren't any bullets left in your gun. You shot them all at my husband, you stupid, stupid little bitch.*

Pearl shoved the head back into the sack, and turned to Hunch. "Put her in a nightgown."

Authors' Notes and Acknowledgements

Newport's reputation as a "sin city" had its roots in the 1880's, when small time gambling and prostitution houses sprang up to satisfy the desires of the U. S. Army soldiers stationed there. Even after the army finished relocating to nearby Ft. Thomas in the mid-1890's, the soldiers came back to Newport by streetcar to visit their favorite saloons and disorderly houses. Once those saloons were equipped with telephones, bookmaking on horse races became a profitable cottage industry.

Because of its geographical positioning—cut off from the state capitol and the rest of Kentucky by hills and bad roads, and across the river from Ohio—Northern Kentucky flourished not only as a hideaway for criminals on the run during the early 1900's, but also as a hotbed of racketeering. Conditions were perfect, when Prohibition arrived, for "Little Mexico", as the region was called, to become the headquarters for a major bootlegging ring.

By the time Prohibition ended, Little Mexico had developed into one of the country's major centers for big time gambling operations. This continued until the 1960's, when *The Saturday Evening Post* ran a feature exposé on Newport, and U.S. Attorney General Robert Kennedy called it a town "long known nationally for wide-open gambling and prostitution...where a lack of public interest had allowed the cash register of organized crime to clang loudly."

In the early 1960's, when the Switch to Honesty Party was elected to city government, things finally got too hot for the Cleveland Syndicate, and the casino owners moved their operations to Las Vegas. Newport was virtually closed down overnight.

The history of Little Mexico and the actions of its outlaw inhabitants gets so convoluted and intertwined, that all motives (logical or otherwise) can't be explained easily in one book. For example, it wasn't until years after the September 21, 1943 surprise raid on the casinos, that attorney Charles E. Lester's motives for the double-cross became known. It came down to greed. Since Lester didn't think his retainer with the Cleveland Syndicate was large enough to match what he thought he was worth, he threw in with Pete Schmidt. Schmidt (the casino owner Lester had previously helped the Syndicate oust from the Beverly Hills Country Club) had vowed revenge and had a plan to get back at the Cleveland Syndicate. His campaign was carried out into the mid-1950's, and this story, among others, will be continued in future novels in the Little Mexico series.

The stories told by Pete Schmidt and Gabbie are true—though Gabbie is a fictional character, and the Joseph Hotel is a fictional place.

Certain practices really did exist, such as putting people into Newport nightgowns and "dingdonging" casino lobbies. The Oasis is a fictional place, but operating a lookout for possible raiders and rigging the club so gambling equipment could be quickly hidden away were common practices that have not only been documented but were also described to the authors in direct eyewitness accounts.

It has also been well documented that almost all city officials and police personnel were on the take. Detective Steve Pope is fictional, though he represents several policemen who, over the years, tried to expose the corruption.

The following characters are also fictional:

Nick Cavanaugh, the Jules Family (and the rest of the cast at The Oasis); Bruno Carpella, Manny, and Al; "Dandy" Charlie DePalma; Jimmy "the Shiv" Turelli; Sophie and her girls (Claudette and Millie); and Detective Virgil Ducker.

Sometimes in searching for answers as to why events took place, authors run up against a brick wall. This is the case with Acting Chief of Police George Gugel. Why was he on duty at the time of the midnight raid on the casinos? Since when does the boss draw the graveyard shift? The authors couldn't find any public records to enlighten them and, not having access to Chief Gugel, came up with the following conjecture. The wartime need for military personnel could have left the Newport police short of manpower, making it necessary for Gugel to take a turn in the shift rotations. There is no way to prove this theory, but the fact remains that, according to the newspaper accounts, Acting Chief Gugel was the officer on duty at the time the order was given to raid the nightspots.

The remaining historical characters (aside from those mentioned above) are: Red Masterson; The Big Four of the Cleveland Syndicate: Sam Tucker, Moe Dalitz, Louis Rothkopf, and Morris Kleinman; independent casino operators Buck Brady, "Sleepout Louie" Levinson, and Jimmy Brink.

The authors wish to thank:

Jason Larson, Curator of Northern Kentucky University's Special Collections and Archives, and Angie Graziani, Executive Assistant for giving access to their extensive collection of newspaper files dealing with the gambling activities in Northern Kentucky; Robert Hahn, Library Director of the *Cincinnati Post*, for providing *The Saturday Evening Post* (March 26, 1960) article: "Kentucky's Open City", and the *Cincinnati Post* (July 3, 1980) article: "Sin City's Reputation Dies Hard"; Larry Trapp, for showing the authors his extensive collection of memorabilia from the casino days of Little Mexico and for the loan of his private collection of newspaper articles, advertisements, and photographs; Wayne and Betty Dammert for sharing their stories. Both worked at The Beverly Hills during the late 1950's—Wayne as a blackjack dealer in the pit, and Betty (a former Radio City Music Hall Rockette) as a dancer in the Beverly Hills chorus line.

Additional thanks to: Rick Combs, Chief Deputy Sheriff of the Clermont County, Ohio Sheriff's office, for his expert advice on police procedures; Ryck Neube for his criticial reading of the manuscript and helpful suggestions; and Lorraine Gibbs for her enthusiastic support.

Four books provided a wealth of information: *RAZZLE DAZZLE* (1995) and *SYNDICATE WIFE* (1968), both written by Hank Messick, reporter for the *Louisville Courier Journal* (1956-63); *INSIDE THE BEVERLY HILLS SUPPER CLUB FIRE* (1996), an eyewitness account by Wayne Dammert and Ronald E. Elliott; and *NEWPORT, KENTUCKY: A Bicentennial History* (1996) edited by Thomas L. Purvis, with coauthors Kenneth M. Clift, Betty Maddox Daniels, Elizabeth Purser Fennell, and Michael E. Whitehead.